P9-DBQ-727

CAMP MURDERFACE

CAMP MURDERFACE

JOSH BERK &
SAUNDRA MITCHELL

HARPER
An Imprint of HarperCollins*Publishers*

Camp Murderface

Map by Corina Lupp

www.harpercollinschildrens.com

Library of Congress Control Number: 2019956240
ISBN 978-0-06-287163-3

Typography by Corina Lupp
20 21 22 23 24 PC/LSCH 10 9 8 7 6 5 4 3 2 1
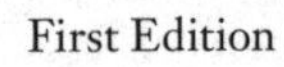
First Edition

To Z Brewer and D. Potter,

Having a blast at camp; wish you were here!

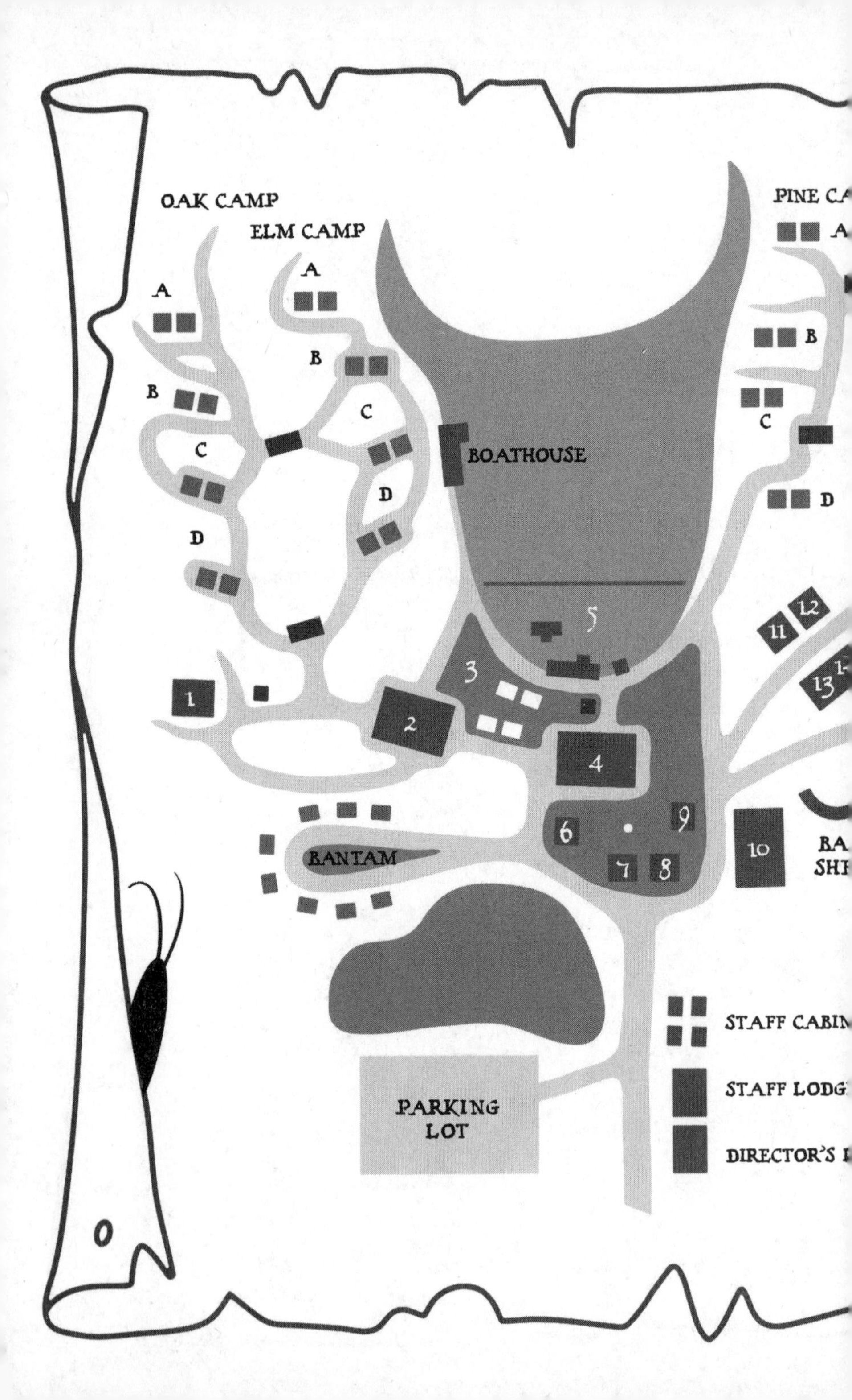
OAK CAMP
ELM CAMP
PINE
A
B
C
D
BOATHOUSE
1
2
3
4
5
6
7
8
9
10
11
12
13
BANTAM
PARKING
LOT
STAFF
STAFF
DIRECTOR'S

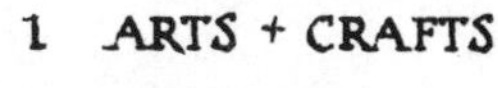

ARCHERY
RANGE

1 ARTS + CRAFTS
2 REC BARN
3 TENNIS/VOLLEYBALL/ATHLETICS
4 GREAT HALL
5 DOCK + DIVING
6 CANTEEN
7 INFIRMARY
8 LAUNDRY
9 LIBRARY
10 EQUIPMENT/STORAGE
11 RADIO STATION
12 PHOTO/DARKROOM
13 TECHNOLOGY LAB

LAWN
WATER
CAMP BUILDING
CABIN
SHOWER/LATRINE

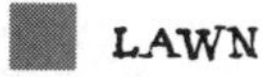

1

Bowl Cut and Chickenlips

June 6, 1983

Corryn

Summer truly starts the minute you can no longer see your parents waving goodbye.

I wave longer than anyone else. A dark thought runs through my mind. *This is the last time I'll see them together.* They're standing there with these big lying smiles. I can see the white of their teeth from a hundred yards away. Like everything is fine—*better than fine!* It's not.

It's not fine.

We used to go to Grandpa's farm in the summer. Back then, we'd wave and wave goodbye, long past the time the old house became a bird-sized speck on the horizon. Now I'm going to camp. And my parents think I don't know it's because they're getting divorced. I wave because I have to, but I don't miss them. I'm not *going* to miss them either. They don't deserve it.

Elliot on the other hand? Elliot, I'll miss.

The night before we left, I even gave him a kiss. It wasn't our first, but it was the longest and saddest one we've shared. I felt tears pop up in my eyes as I kissed him, and believe me, I'm not the kind of girl who cries easily.

My friend Joy from school will cry if she forgets her homework or gets a B on a spelling test. I didn't cry even when I wiped out and sprained both my wrists. Plus, I always get As on spelling tests. Consistent. C-O-N-S-I-S-T-E-N-T. Consistent.

But nine weeks away from Elliot, that's worse than a million sprained wrists. That's like spraining both my wrists and both my ankles and splitting my head open on a rock. Oh, I'm gonna miss him so much! So . . . the night before camp I bent down and leaned in and kissed him.

Right on the handlebars.

I can't believe they won't let me bring my bike to camp! Why can't you bring a bike to camp? Elliot doesn't take up much room. He can sleep in the corner!

Or he can have the sleeping bag and *I'll* sleep in the corner!

Alas, no. I'll be out here for *nine* weeks without him. I hope I don't forget how to ride.

Elliot really is a beautiful bike. He's matte black and bright gold, with twenty-inch mag wheels, racing tires, and a slick silver stripe down the side. It's a BMX racing bike, just like you see Danny Stark riding in all the magazines. He's been the world BMX champion for three years running now (although his 1981 win was controversial).

All I'm saying is, if a quad reverse bunny hop over the finish line is wrong, I don't want to be right.

I literally had to beg on hands and knees for Elliot. Hands and knees. Mom and Dad were not cool at all about it. Not cool at all. It was like they were trying to outdo each other with who could be more *un*cool. I'd have to say that particular contest ended in a tie. It's too dangerous, they said. Too expensive. They had a million reasons. What they really meant is that it's not for girls.

They're wrong. But I finally got Elliot (note to self: Was Elliot a divorce-guilt present?) and now I have to leave him for a whole summer. He couldn't even ride all the way to camp with me.

All the kids going to Camp Sweetwater got dropped off at the rest stop parking lot. We stood around trying to look cool while we waited for the camp transport to roll in. It was wall-to-wall kids and parents and weepy goodbyes, so there was no cool.

There were little baby primary kids, and in-between kids like me, and teenagers, like that guy with the almost mustache. I don't know who he's kidding. It's going to take him fifty years to turn that thing into a Tom Selleck.

Five buses, badly painted white and squeaking like no tomorrow, trundled into the parking lot. Somebody has stenciled CAMP SWEETWATER on the sides in red. The paint had run, leaving the words dripping down the sides like blood.

I tried to point this out to my parents, but they were too busy making sure I had plenty of underwear and suntan lotion and pretending to be totally, completely, absolutely not about to break up our home. Well, whatever happens, at least I'll have custody of Elliot.

Counselors poured off the buses and sorted us by grade. After granting us one last farewell, they herded us into our sketchy rides in grade order.

The lineup is simple: two buses each of little kids

and middles, and one for the teens. When I jump into my seat, it pukes up crumbly, gritty foam. Awesome.

The road to camp twists its way through the trees, and it feels too narrow for the bus. The bus bounces and rattles and shakes like we're driving over the surface of the moon. What kind of shocks are on this thing? The noise shakes up the swarm of butterflies in my stomach.

I don't know anybody here and I don't think anyone else does, either. It's weirdly quiet. Not like going to school, where people trade seats and lean over to talk and throw stuff when the driver's not looking. Here, we mostly stare at each other, then look away real fast.

A couple kids seem like they're just barely holding back tears. There's a girl with a huge cliff of bangs towering over her forehead, a style my dad calls "case of hairspray." She's scribbling furiously on some stationery. Is she writing a letter to the people she just saw twenty minutes ago?

There's a boy with dark hair and dark eyes and a big smile, nose in a book, reading intently like there is going to be a test. Is there going to be a test? I try to sneak a glance at the cover but get interrupted.

A very tall teenage girl—one of the counselors, judging by the name tag on her Cure T-shirt—hops up and starts shouting at us from the front of the bus. She has a megaphone, like a cheerleader would use.

"Right, then," she says in a heavy British accent. She sounds like a lady in a James Bond movie. I figure she's doing a funny voice so I shout back "Right!" in my own British accent. Unfortunately, I'm the only one who does. My cheeks burn a little. Whatever.

She continues. "My name is Mary, innit? And some of you lot are lucky enough to have me as your counselor for the next nine weeks. I know I look like a sweetheart . . ."

Okay, not doing an accent. Actually British. Got it.

Here she pauses and blinks her big, blue-mascaraed eyelashes at us. "I'm a counselor. I'm not your mum and I'm not here to wipe your bum."

The kid with the book laughs loudly, but no one else does. This Mary is a little scary. Scary Mary.

"Which one of you lot is Corryn?" she asks.

Now I really feel my cheeks burn. I raise my hand and feel the eyes of all the campers lock on to me.

"That'd be me," I say.

"Take better care of your things, Corryn," she says.

"These fell out of your sack when you were getting on the bus."

She holds up a pair of underwear. *My* underwear. The ones with blue bunnies on them. The ones my mom had written CORRYN QUINN on with permanent marker across the elastic. Great, now she's trying to ruin my life two different ways.

Scary Mary fires the undies at me like a kid shooting rubber bands in math class. They land in the next seat, right in the lap of the kid with the book. He hands them to me like it's no big deal. Like he's just passing a stack of papers back in class.

"My mom writes my name in my underwear too," he says with a shrug. Then the goober introduces himself. "I'm Tez. Tez Jones."

"I'm Corryn," I say, feeling like my throat is on fire. "But you already knew that."

Tez

Everything at Camp Sweetwater is chaos. Or it could be entropy.

It's hard to say which because I haven't been here long enough to know what the natural state is. Whichever it is, my current state is somewhat unnatural. I currently know exactly one person, and that's Corryn from the bus. We had an actual conversation, a good portent for this summer.

Unfortunately, other portents are more negative. Mary, the British counselor, has replicated.

Gavin, who is Mary in male form, drags us middle boys to one side of the flagpole. I can only hope they won't spawn any further.

There are knots of kids scattered all over the front drive. Tall trees surround the gravel roads and paths at the entrance. Near the Director's Lodge, there's a paved parking lot, but it's overgrown with low, heavy bushes and scrubby trees.

Counselors and camp directors and other official-looking people group us by age, then by camp, then by cabin.

With each separation, I try to wave at Corryn, but she's studying the sky. There's nothing up there but altocumulus clouds—white, fluffy ones, well-spaced. If she's trying to tell the weather, it's a waste of time. Altocumulus clouds just mean pleasantness, although it might also have rained yesterday.

It would be nice if we were in the same group. I could

tell her all about clouds and precipitation. However, the chances of that seem to be dwindling.

From what I can tell from the *Camper's Guidebook*, there should be about a hundred fifty of us here, give or take. It seems like way more as we swelter under the sun on the lawn, but as we get separated into smaller units, the numbers make sense. Eight cabins per camp, four people per cabin, plus the baby camp . . . yep, the numbers make sense.

Lake Sweetwater sits smack in the middle of everything, vaguely horseshoe-shaped. The littlest kids go into the Bantam Camp, right off the big path. It's closest to the main buildings, like the Great Hall and the Rec Barn, and the infirmary. The seniors—the high school kids—drift toward the paths to the east.

That leaves all the rest of us to head to junior camp, along the west side of the lake.

"Hopkiss, Johnson, Jones, Kwan," Gavin yells. His voice breaks, and a lot of people giggle. I feel kind of bad for him, but I pretend to giggle anyway. That way, I look like everybody else. That is *paramount*.

I just want to be a regular kid this summer, 100 percent normal. No "Poor Tez" or "Watch-out-for-Tez" or "It's what makes you special, Tez."

That last one, honestly, is the absolute worst.

The four of us shuffle with our bags again and find ourselves in a cluster, just us.

"Oak Camp," Gavin growls, getting his voice as low as possible after that squeak. "Cabin Group A."

According to the camp map, that puts us the farthest away from everything. We're tucked at the upper northwest end of the lake. Past our cabins is nothing but primal forest. That could be cool or terrifying, depending.

Cool, I decide. It's going to be *cool.* But it would be cooler with a friend.

"All right, you little mingers," Gavin says, waving his clipboard at us. "I'm your counselor. When I call your name, I'd advise you speak up. Anyone left behind spends the summer in the woods with the wolves."

I raise my hand. "There are no wolves left in Ohio. They were hunted to extinction in the early 1800s, along with the bobcats. There are coyotes and foxes. But they're afraid of people."

From the look on Gavin's face, he is definitely thrilled to have all the facts. He approaches me. "What's your name?"

Just to be on the safe side, I lean over his clipboard before he can try to read my full name out loud, and point to it. "I'm Tez. Tez Jones."

"Right," Gavin says. "From here on out, you're Chickenlips."

I start to say that chickens don't have lips, but Gavin palms my entire face. His hand smells like sweat and his fingers are really hot. Since this probably means shut up, I do.

Moving on, Gavin calls out Chun Kwan. He takes one look at him and says, "Nostrils."

Completely baffling; Chun's nose is about as ordinary as a nose can get. This doesn't matter to Gavin; he keeps going. Next on the list is Graham Hopkiss—Gavin dubs him Bowl Cut. It's an extremely fair name; he has an awesome bowl cut. It's shiny, auburn, and geometrically precise.

(Nostrils has soft, black feathers like Rob Lowe, and the other kid has a tight, boxy fade. This whole cabin has great hair, if you ask me.)

"Ryan Johnson," Gavin says, and doesn't even look up.

Warily, Ryan raises his hand.

Gavin looks him over, then rolls his eyes. "Hm. I'm calling you Knees. Look at you, just standing there with your knees."

"Everyone has knees," Ryan points out.

"Shut it, Knees," Gavin says. "Or I'll change it to something else that everyone's got!"

Nostrils and Bowl Cut snicker. Clearly they've thought of something else Gavin could call Knees. I wonder if it's Appendix. Or Pancreas. Pancreas would be hilarious.

Gavin's not interested in hilarious. "So, like I said, you're Oak Camp, Cabin Group A. No tradesies, no takesy-backsies, no transfers. Learn it, love it, get used to it!"

As we trade incredulous looks, Gavin barks out rules, which is unnecessary. We all have the *Camper's Guidebook*. Also, the rules are pretty simple:

We eat with our cabin group, we have activities with our cabin group . . .

"You shower with your cabin group," Gavin bellows.

Staggering into Bowl Cut, Nostrils laughs. "Our cabin *group*? Oh wow, man. We're showering with the girls!"

"Your gob!" Gavin says. "Shut it!"

Nostrils and Bowl Cut snicker behind their hands. This counts as shut gobs, apparently, because Gavin goes on.

"So, right, then. *No* phone calls home. Pay phone doesn't work; you can buy stamps at the camp store. Moving on! Every bloody cabin's collecting beads. Brilliant bants? Earn a bead. Act like a tosser? Lose a bead. Spend them up at the end of camp for color war advantages. Clear?"

We all nod to agree that we're clear, but I look to Nostrils and Knees. We're definitely not clear. From context clues, it sounds like beads are extremely important. Possibly they're even a disciplinary tool. I'm sure this will clarify itself. I make a mental note to watch for additional bead context.

As Gavin continues, the rest of his instructions get closer to American English. Swimming test before we can swim, no boats without supervision, sign-outs for equipment, etcetera, etcetera. I know there are going to be special restrictions for me, but I'm not going to worry about that. I always have extra rules. I just need to make sure no one else knows about them.

Restless, I start to bend at the knees. I'm wobbly and rubbery under the hot sun and the dull tirade.

Looking around, I know I'm not the only one. Oak Camp Cabin Group A is *not* paying attention. But we *are* listening—to Gavin's accent. Bowl Cut is already trying to imitate it.

I'm going to wait until I have a better sample size. I try to focus on Gavin's words. Like, keenly focus, with all my attention. I keep getting distracted though, because he sounds like the bad guys in every movie ever. Also, he kinda acts like one.

After he threatens us a couple more times, he tells us to pick up our gear. We're hiking to Cabin Group A, and we'd better stick to the path or get eaten by wolves. Gavin seems really dedicated to the idea of wolves so I'm going to let that one go.

Hefting my bag, I take one last look at Corryn. She crosses her eyes at me, so I pretend to stick a finger up my nose. We both smile at the same time.

I mouth to her, "Group A?"

Her smile fades, and she mouths back, "Group C. Sorry."

So much for a first friend on the first day.

2
Is That a Bug?

Corryn

Group C; that seems like a good omen. *C* is for Corryn! *C* is for yes, if you speak Spanish. *C* is for cookie; I heckin' love cookies.

What I don't heckin' love is that it takes fifteen buggy, muggy minutes just to get to Oak Camp Group C. We walk past *another* perfectly *good* camp to get there. With each step, the trees get thicker, and we get farther and farther away from everything.

Like, hello; by the time we get to the Great Hall for lunch, will there even be any food left? I'm extremely concerned about that situation. I like food. I like it a *lot.*

C is also for concerning—the last *open* shower-slash-latrine was five minutes ago. The one closest to our cabin group is boarded up. Literally—boards are nailed over the doors and windows. I knew they were pulling this camp out of mothballs, but come on, people! It figures that Mom and Dad would throw me into the first lousy place they found, just to get rid of me.

Dust puffs up on the dirt-and-gravel path as we walk, a whole cloud of it. The air is a haze of gnats so thick I'm picking them from my teeth. We're going to be filthy by the time we walk back from our showers. Not that I care about being dirty. I'm just saying, it makes no sense.

We finally arrive at Group C and I'm ready for a C-esta. The other campers in Oak probably are too. We watch A and B march on up the main trail, even deeper into the woods than we are. Maybe I'm imagining it, but I swear I can hear that kid Tez talking about some kind of tick bite that makes you allergic to meat.

Mega weird! I hope I get the chance to ask him about it later.

I drop my bag in the dirt outside our cabin, right next to my new roommates' stuff. Already, they chat like friends. They wave their arms, laughing at jokes they didn't share with me. I can't help but feel like an intruder, like I'm sneaking around someplace I don't belong. I try to shake it off and join the fun.

"I'm Corryn!" I announce to them.

At first, they don't respond. Then one of the girls laughs.

"We know," she says. "Your panties told us."

"Ew, panties," says the blonde with the shag haircut.

My face burns like I already have a summer's worth of sun. This is stupid. "Ew" girl's face is stupid. This cabin is stupid.

I don't want to be here! Dad said it would be fun; Mom said I needed to spend more time with people instead of bikes. And yet, I know it's because they want me away while they do their dirty work. It's their Summer of Separation. Do they really think I don't know?

I think they don't, but they might have suspected. They gave me hush money. A bribe. Five bucks a week for the camp canteen, the same as my allowance. It's like a bonus: no washing dishes, but still the bucks roll in.

If I save up all summer, I'll have forty-five bucks. Forty-five dollars will put new mag wheels on Elliot. That's all I have to look forward to; that's why I finally agreed. But when I imagined camp, I left out the part where I would be marooned in another state without my dad, who makes camping awesome.

My cabinmates shuffle aimlessly. It's not obvious if we're supposed to go in, or wait, or what. In fact, except for walking up the path to the cabin, we had zero information whatsoever. The short girl tries to peer into one of the windows, but they're still a good foot above her head. Sneak-out-proof. Clever.

Finally, Mary comes up the trail behind us, already yelling.

"What's this, some kind of hen party?" she demands. "Waiting for your butler? Well, there ISN'T one!"

"We were waiting for you," says the girl with intricately braided hair.

"What for? I'm not your mummy, Braids," says Mary, shooting daggers with her eyes. Quickly, her gaze cuts across us. She points to the smallest girl and says, "You're Ew." Then she turns to the one with the sky-high bangs and perfect feathers. "Hello, Hairspray."

Mary sure loves the nicknames. I wonder if she knows that *she* has one. *'Allo, Scary Mary, emphasis on the Scary, pip pip, Bob's your uncle, here's the loo!* Probably not, since I've only called her that in my head. Definitely not saying it out loud. I can't be the only one thinking it, though.

I brace for my nickname, but Mary looks right through me. I don't want her making fun of me, I really don't. But not getting a nickname is somehow *more* insulting.

"Get a move on!" Scary Mary yells.

O-kay, then! Pulling open the cabin's rickety door, I survey the place I'm going to be living in for the next nine weeks. Dang. Nine weeks. I try to reframe it in my mind. I'm living here for forty-five buckeroonies. This is time served in my sweet, sweet Elliot's best interest. Don't think about anything else. Just mag wheels. *Mag wheels.* Yes. Okay. I can definitely do this.

Door, open.

And here's what the place looks like: two bunk beds, one on either side, decked with bare plastic mattresses waiting for our bedding. Cubbies fill the space between the beds, next to built-in desks. A lone little air freshener dangles from the ceiling. Winter Forest isn't doing much to chase away the smell of *used cabin*, to be honest.

The walls have been scrubbed clean, old wood pretending to be new. The back wall is super shadowy—

and right in the middle, it's almost black. The shadow suddenly *shifts* on the wall and the hair on my arms stands up.

What's happening here?

Dark spirals spin from the shadow, a pulsing bull's-eye that grows and churns. It spreads to cover the back wall in ever-thickening lines of black. For a minute, it looks like an invisible, deranged child is scribbling with a handful of crayons.

Gulp.

Looks like *C* is also for creepy.

And crawly.

And cockroaches.

And centipedes. The wall isn't black—it's alive!

Every bug I've ever seen—earwigs and beetles and spiders and ticks. They're humming and crawling and buzzing and surging.

I'm not afraid of bugs. I'll squish a millipede with the heel of my bare foot on the bathroom floor without blinking. But this isn't *a* bug. It's not even ten.

It's *thousands.*

Teeming over the windows, they blot out the sunlight. As the cabin darkens, the bugs course up the ceiling. Like a black mold, they spread. When they reach the bare light fixture, they fall. It's a storm of insects, raining onto the floor as more emerge from dark corners.

I shouldn't be able to hear them, but I swear I *can*. Millions of tiny feet, tiny pincers, tiny claws, *click-click-click*, all over everything. My stomach threatens to hurl at the *sound* of them, hundreds of thousands, ticking across the cabin.

They spread fast. Faster.

"Bail!" I shout as I back out the door. "Everybody bail!"

"Wrong bloody way, You," Mary barks.

She shoves somebody, and all of a sudden, I'm in the cabin with the girl she named Ew. I think her actual, for-real name is Tammi, and the only reason I'm thinking about that is because the swarm washes toward us. There are so many of them, they scramble and climb over each other. There are dunes of bugs. Ripples. Waves.

The second I stop thinking about Ew's real name, my brain goes hog wild. The mass hasn't reached me yet, but it's close. There are just seconds until I have centipedes in my hair, roaches in my ears. Ants marching into my nose and beetles rushing down my throat.

For a moment, I'm dying, choking to death on spiders that scrabble across my tongue and ticks that pierce my throat. It's way too easy to imagine them skittering over my whole body, devouring me to the bones.

That's what bugs do to bodies. They eat us. They eat us down to the skeleton.

I gag and yell, "Mary!"

"Ew!" says Ew before her eyes focus.

When they do, she lets out a shriek. It's impressive, because she's way tiny and that scream is way big. Her high-pitched howl doesn't scare the bugs away. In fact, the black wave moves faster. It's like the sound excited them. *Attracted* them.

Tiny bodies spill on the floor and swarm up the bunks.

They're coming for us.

They're coming right at us.

Without thinking, I turn and shove Ew out of the cabin. I'm right on her heels, and the two of us crash into Scary Mary.

"Close the door," I say with authority and not a spot of terror in my voice. Nope. None. Not at all. "It's full of bugs!"

This sets Scary Mary off. She seems to double in size

when she takes a gigantic, T-shirt-stretching breath. Then she starts screaming.

"It's camp, you nitwit! You're gonna see a bug! Guess what: you might also see a speck of dirt and a blade of grass! If that's not okay with you bloody princesses, I suggest you gather up your tiaras right now and head back to your mummies to live in one of those plastic bubbles!"

Okay, then, *don't* close the door, Scary Mary! And since she doesn't, I bail, like, just full-out book it to escape. That's when Braids and Hairspray see the massing, gleaming sea of black and brown heading right for them.

Their shrieks meld with Ew's. They're a siren, ringing out again and again.

Then, much to my satisfaction, Mary takes one look inside our cabin. She turns a pale, mossy green and bolts.

Her scream follows her down the path, flip-flops flapping on her callusy feet. I've seriously never seen anybody run that fast in flops. It's like Roadrunner had a speed baby with the Tasmanian Devil and that baby went for a pedicure.

Bending down, I pick up a big old rock and wing it

at the cabin door. A cloud of dust explodes when it hits the wood at the corner. The door slams shut.

Are we safe? Probably not.

But is it better?

Way, yeah.

Tez

Halfway through unpacking our stuff, the British girls' counselor comes huffing into our cabin.

She looks us over with disdain, really English disdain. Like somebody used the wrong fork at dinner and it's killing her not to say something, because saying something would be even ruder than using the wrong fork.

"Where's Gavin?" she finally asks, her nostrils curled.

We've been at camp for thirty minutes; we can't possibly smell bad yet! Although to be fair, the walk up the west side of the lake lasted for seventeen minutes, thirty-four seconds, according to my new watch. It wasn't a short jog.

Also, I'm pretty sure we're not supposed to have girls in our cabin (100 percent sure; it's on page fourteen of the *Camper's Guidebook*.) I don't know if that applies to counselors, but it seems like it should.

Nevertheless, Nostrils points outside. "Out back. Taking a nature break."

She rolls her eyes and disappears. Not a minute later, Gavin comes through the door. Now *he's* annoyed, and his disdain is more like an angry soccer coach's. Or a *football* coach's, to be perfectly accurate, since he probably calls soccer football.

"Drop what you're doing and come on," he barks, then walks back outside.

We follow the command, because what else are we going to do? It's not like we're *that* excited about putting our shampoo in the cubbies.

As soon as I realized there were no dressers, I made my summer plan. Half the suitcase for dirty, half for clean, carefully rotated. Fresh socks on the top, always. Mom wants me to change socks at least twice a day.

According to Dad, she's worried about trench foot. When he said that, Mom gave him a dirty look, and he laughed, so probably there was something else going on there.

(Trench foot, by the way, is an immersion syndrome. That just means it's something that happens when your feet get wet and stay wet. First you get blisters, then sores, then the flesh on your feet starts to rot, and you can lose all of your toes. In fact, you can lose your whole foot if you get gangrene! Well, you don't just lose it. Somebody has to cut it off. It doesn't fall off on its own, like your toes do.)

We march down the main trail, then branch off onto a smaller path. There, we're greeted by the camp director. I know this for a fact because she claps her hands when she sees us and she says, "Hello, boys! I'm your camp director, Mrs. Gladys Winchelhauser!"

She's one of those medium ages, where I can't tell if she's young or old. Her hair is blond or maybe sort of gray. A deep smile shows off either perfect teeth or perfect dentures. The clapping and enthusiasm are undatable; they go with her uniform of khaki shorts and camp T-shirt.

She points at us and gestures down the path. "Hup, hup, hup! We need all your big, strong muscles to help us move the girls from Group C to the empty cabin in your group."

"Why?" I ask.

Mrs. Winchelhauser's smile does not fade. But her voice is less cheerful. "We thought it was ready for campers, but it's not quite there yet. We're reopening after a . . . hiatus. Thus we're still working out a few kinks."

As I try to figure out how a *cabin* can be broken, the path widens and opens into C Group. There are two cabins here. One is pretty run down, and I can see why they wouldn't want to put anybody in there. But the other one looks fine. In fact, it looks a little nicer than ours.

Just as I'm about to point this out, I see the girls grouped in the middle of the clearing. Including one I recognize. I break into a smile, a sparkly kind of lightness lifting me from the inside.

Throwing up a hand, I wave and call out, "Corryn!"

All four girls turn to look at me at the same time. Three of them seem suspicious, but Corryn smiles. She doesn't wave back. She's too cool for that. She throws a thumbs-up.

Wow! I don't know what happened to her cabin, but it's good luck for me! If we're in the same group, we'll share most of our activity times. Potential first friend at camp: back in action!

"If you gentlemen would be kind enough to help these young ladies with their bags, they can hurry and settle in before our first activity."

Mrs. Winchelhauser's voice is upbeat and sunny, like it's perfectly ordinary to move a whole cabin on the very first day of camp. Also, it seems to me like the girls carried their own bags to camp in the first place. They should be able to carry them from one bunk to another, but okay. Maybe this is one of those "unspoken social rules" my dad says we all need to learn.

That being the case, I walk right over to Corryn. "Is this one yours?"

She gives me a dubious look. "Yeah, but . . ."

I haul it up, throwing the strap over my shoulder. I even manage to counterbalance the weight so I don't go careening off and fall down. I'm playing this exceptionally cool. "Guess what? You're going to be in my group now."

"Yeah?" she says but doesn't elaborate.

We move out first, hiking up the short trail beneath the cool shade of the trees on either side of us.

It's really pretty out, kind of like camp decided to give us the perfect first day. Birds call over the lake, and a gentle breeze kisses our skin. When we step into patches of sunlight, it's instantly warm and the air tastes like summer. This is going to be the best nine weeks ever.

Behind us, I hear Bowl Cut say, "Is that a bug?" and one of the girls shrieks.

Laughing, I say, "I hope she doesn't do that every time she sees an insect."

"There are . . . *circumstances*," Corryn informs me flatly. "Winchelhauser says there must be a nest under our cabin, because it was full of bugs. Billions of them. Like, ankle deep."

With a laugh, I start to say she has to be exaggerating. But she gives me the evilest eye in the world, and I realize *she means it.* Ankle-deep bugs? Gross. I give an involuntary shudder and ask, "What kind?"

"Well, that's the weird part," Corryn says, as I lead her to the empty cabin in Group A. She walks up to the door and stares at it hard. Then, like she's summoning up all her courage, she yanks it open.

When she does, it reveals . . . an empty cabin. The twin of mine, with the same bunks and cubbies, green plastic mattresses and all. Corryn exhales slowly, then holds the door open wider, and I carry her bag in.

As I drop it, I ask, "What was the weird part, exactly?"

Corryn sits on the edge of her new bunk. She doesn't seem scared. More like disconcerted. Like something is wrong, but she can't quite put her finger on it. Screwing up her face, she finally says, "It was all different bugs. I counted at least ten kinds. And some of them were the kinds that eat each other. It couldn't be just one nest."

My skin crawls. "You're totally right. That can't be. But there has to be a logical explanation."

"I guess," she says skeptically. At least, those are her words. Her expression says something else entirely. It's plain as day; it says: *You don't believe me. I get that. But trust me—it wasn't right.*

The pure, clear certainty in her brown eyes makes me doubt. Maybe there *wasn't* a rational explanation. Maybe it was a sign. An omen.

A harbinger.

Shaking that thought out of my head, I get out of the way for the rest of my cabinmates. Creepy stories are 100 percent part of camp life, or so I've read. Perhaps Corryn's just getting an early start. A daylight start. Yes. That's what this is, for sure.

I take one more look at her; her expression hasn't changed. I rub my arms and step into the sun. This is fine. It's totally fine, I tell myself.

I really wish I believed me.

3
A Tale of Two Hearts

Corryn

If the bugvasion traumatized Scary Mary, she totally doesn't show it.

She climbs onto one of the picnic tables, then shouts into her megaphone. She's like a cheerleader for nightmares. "Listen up, you filthy little pukes! Hope you've got your"—I swear she looks at me—"big-kid knickers on, because this is how it's gonna go!"

We stare up at her as she sweats and smacks at the bugs circling around her. There are mosquitoes the size of hens around here and they are hungry for blood. This is *not* what my dad meant when he said camp would be an opportunity to get back to nature.

"*First*, you're going to stay on the trails or get left behind!" Scary Mary says. "And while you're out here, get some wood for the fire. We'll get a proper bonfire going tonight and it will be lovely. Provided that one of you lot knows how to light a fire.

"I personally may have *slightly* misrepresented my level of outdoorsy experience when I applied for this here position," she goes on. "I just really wanted to see the US of A. And yes, maybe there was a thing or two back in London I needed to get away from . . . Right. Off you go!"

I'm not worried about getting a fire started. I've done it lots of times. My dad and I used to do the kind of camping where you don't even have a campsite. "Free camping," he calls it. You just hike around until you find what looks like a decent spot and set up. I loved doing that with him.

"The closer you get to real matter," he would insist, like he was personally Jack Kerouac instead of just quoting him like his biggest, doofiest fan, "rock air fire and wood, boy, the more spiritual the world is."

He doesn't think sleeping in a cabin should even count as camping. Then again, he never met Oak Camp

Cabin Group C, girls' side. There was way too much outdoors in that indoors, even for him.

When my parents are divorced, will camping be how Dad and I spend our one weekend together a month? What'll *that* be like?

Anyway.

So, yeah, I know about fire. I know all about how you need bigger logs underneath and smaller dry sticks to start the fire crackling. I know all about stacking them in a way to let the air flow through to feed the flames. I know that tons of smoke will ward off bugs too. Bring on the fire!

"Mush," Mary says.

Mush? Like we're dogs?

"Um, quick question," I say. "How do you want us to carry the wood?"

"In your arms, love. With your hands that God gave you. Like people did for millions of years. Do you think people who used to live here had chainsaws and lorries? Do you think they had golf carts? Is that what you want? You want me to bring you a golf cart, duchess?"

I know enough to say nothing in response.

"A bit of twine might be nice," Tez says. Yup. He's

the kind of kid who knows everything *except* when to say nothing.

"Oh, you think Indians had a nice bit of twine when they gathered wood around these parts two hundred years ago?" Scary Mary says with a vicious laugh.

"Sure," Tez says, unfazed. "There's no reason to assume the Miami peoples of Ohio wouldn't have rope. Rope and its usage go back to ancient times."

"Well, we're not in bloody ancient times now, are we?"

"I mean, kind of," he says. "If you consider it, if you consider us, from the perspective of future humans who might dwell here eons hence. To the people thousands of years in the future, it is we who are the ancients."

Even the mountains around us roll their eyes.

"Ooh," Tez says. "Can we carry the firewood on our heads like the Luo women do? Lots of people do it, but the Luo are the best. They can carry like seventy percent of their body weight on their heads!"

"You can carry one hundred percent of your body weight atop your bum for all I care. Just get going!"

Scary Mary has a small knife in her hand, and consequently, we do as we are told.

We don't really have to hike far to find wood. There

are fallen limbs all over camp, including across the trails. Did I mention this place barely looks open? But I don't mind stretching my legs a bit. These paths would be wicked on a bike. I imagine the jumps I could nail. I miss Elliot.

Wandering a bit, I stray from the path and leave the group behind. I have a decent armload of branches of various sizes, and decide for fun to try balancing them on my head. They slide off and tumble down my back. One snags my shirt. But I'm nothing if not persistent. I try again. And again.

I can only balance one or two sticks on my head at a time, but I feel proud that I can navigate the hike while mastering this old-fashioned art. It *would* be nice to have some twine. That Tez sure knows a lot about rope.

For a while, I just walk, confident I can find my way back. I've always been good at finding my way home. With the branches in my arms—and a few on my head—I feel like I will definitely contribute to the fire. I'm about to turn around when I hear the *blub* of something splashing in the lake.

I walk closer to the water's edge. It's a duck—no, two ducks. Splashing happily. Hello, duckies. Then a stick near the water's edge catches my eye. It's darker than the rest of the wood I've seen, and gnarled like a knot.

Carefully balancing the sticks on my head, I bend down, keeping my back straight, just dipping from the knees. I pick up the black stick and run my thumb over its cold surface. Its chill seems to seep into my fingers, weird and unsettling. I don't like the way it feels; it almost gives off a hum. Low. Threatening.

Just as I start to throw it back, Scary Mary barks right in my ear. "We're not playing fetch, You!"

Shuddering, I shove it in the middle of my stack and trudge on.

Tez

With the sun going down, and most of the other kids already back at their cabins, the Great Hall looms in long shadows.

Sunset streams through the giant windows as we collect our sack dinners. (Real food service is supposed to start tomorrow. Tonight, it's PB&J, a cup of applesauce, a bag of questionable carrot sticks, a warm pudding cup, and a carton of chocolate milk.)

The sunset's blazing oranges and reds reflect off the

shiny wooden floor and make the stone walls at either end seem to glow. In the middle of each is a blackened fireplace, at least as tall as a first grader. A first grader tall, and probably five first graders wide. The first grader isn't an internationally approved unit of measurement, but that's what I imagine when I see the empty, sooty maws.

Squared wooden arches hold up the ceiling; somebody has splashed a brand-new coat of red paint over both. That same red is all over camp. The showers are painted red, the signs at each camp—red. Even the boathouses at the edge of the lake. It's just a little bit creepy. There must have been a sale on the shade, but somebody should have thought this through.

When the sun dips, the rows of empty tables run with bloody light. Great for the appetite, you know? Sliding onto the bench next to Corryn, I joke, "Who decorated this place? Michael Myers?"

Bowl Cut drops his bag and sits across from us. "Are you guys talking about *Halloween*? Did your parents let you see it?"

"No," I admit, deflated. Horror movies aren't educational, according to my parents. Also, I like to fall asleep without worrying about guys with hockey masks in my closet.

"Who's talking about *Halloween*?" Knees asks, sliding in next to Bowl Cut. "Man, that was righteous. I saw it at the drive-in, double feature with *Friday the 13th*. There were girls screaming *everywhere*."

Corryn unwraps the waxed paper on her sandwich. "I bet it wasn't just the girls."

"Just the girls what?" Ew asks, standing with her bag until Hairspray and Braids decide where to sit. They give me identical stink faces, then finally crowd in next to Nostrils. I guess I messed up boys' side–girls' side, but oh well.

"Horror movies," Knees says, taking a huge bite of his sandwich. Then he keeps talking, his voice muffled by Jif and grape jelly. "My moms lets me see all of them. We have cable, so . . ."

We all murmur in admiration. I think Knees is the only person I know who has cable. Trading a look with Corryn, I can tell even she's impressed. We haven't gotten it yet. It's really expensive and our library has VHS tapes and a VCR we can borrow for free.

"Yeah, like, I've seen *Slumber Party Massacre*, *The Howling*, *Poltergeist*, *The Omen*, all the Jason movies, all the *Halloweens* . . ."

Nostrils snorts. "That's not even real, man."

"No doy, genius." Knees looks at the rest of us like, *Can you guys believe this dork?* Subtly, I shake my head with everybody else. "They're movies!"

Grabbing the bottom of his bag, Nostrils dumps his whole dinner onto the table. His applesauce rolls toward Braids. She pushes it back with one finger, like it might be nuclear waste or something. Nostrils doesn't even notice; he's shaking his head right back at us. "Yeah, well, some real stuff—some real *scary* stuff—went down right here."

"Where?" Ew asks.

"Here," Nostrils says, then points at the floor. "Camp Sweetwater." He looks dumbfounded, his gaze moving from face to face. "You mean you guys don't *know*?"

The Great Hall smells like the cabins, old and woody, but there's something sour and wet underneath it. The whole building creaks, and the unlit wagon-wheel chandeliers sway just enough to throw strange shadows in every direction.

"Let me guess," Corryn says. She waves a carrot stick casually. "Blah blah bandit with a golden arm, somebody stole it, blah blah—" She whips a hand out and grabs my shoulder. "I WANT MY GOLDEN ARM BACK!"

Startled, I jerk and my heart jumps. With seven pairs of eyes trained on me, I do my best to look collected. I'm cool. I wasn't scared. I shove potato chips in my mouth, because I'm afraid if I say anything, my voice might warble.

Nostrils scoffs. "That's more *made-up* stuff. Listen. I'm gonna tell you the real dirt on this place. Don't say I never did anything for you, all right?" He dips his head and lowers his voice to a murmur. Looking at each of us, he says, "Like, two hundred years ago or something, Indians lived around here, right?"

"The Miami peoples," I supply. "They spoke an Algonquian language; they're related to the Lenape and Shawnee."

Knees presses an elbow into my ribs. "Shut up, Chickenlips. Let the man talk."

With that, Hairspray, Braids, and Ew do a wave of rolled eyes at me. Curling my arms around my dinner, I lean into the circle—fully up with the shut.

"Right, so the *Miami peoples*," Nostrils says, picking up where he left off, "lived here and were chill and everything, okay? Then these French dudes showed up. They ran away from Paris because all those fools up in there were cutting off heads and making a mess—"

"That's one way to describe the guillotine," I whisper to Corryn. She smirks and bumps her shoulder against me. Hey, I made her laugh. Ish!

"But the dudes that showed up here were bad news. I'm talking like, robbing and murdering and stealing and . . . yeah, they were like, we don't care if people are already here, this is our lake now.

"The Indians saw them dumping coffins in the lake, like big ones. Metal ones, you know? And they sank to the bottom. And after that, they wouldn't come back—the Miami, I mean. They wouldn't come back; they said the lake was tainted.

"But the French dudes were like, nah, it's good! And they built a house by the water and had like a farm and stuff, but mostly their job was stealing. And they were good at it, right? They couldn't get caught. They'd go and rob a bunch of stuff, and steal horses and whatever, and just come back here and nothing would touch them.

"The sheriffs or whatever, they'd get lost in the woods trying to find them. Or they'd forget about who they were after, what they did, and didn't care or anything.

"And other people, they never wanted to come here. They said there was a bad air in the woods. But sometimes, if they got too close, they'd disappear."

At that, Nostrils smooths his hands against the table. When he leans in, we all do. It's impossible not to watch him, not with more story to hear and that knowing spark in his dark eyes. None of us dare to move. Not a crinkle, crackle, or crunch interrupts his tale.

"Without a trace, you guys. They would just disappear! No bodies or anything were ever found. It was like the ground swallowed them up. The French dudes got older and older, but they never got sick. They never died. But they did vanish after a while. Or maybe people forgot them, just like they forgot about *what they put in the lake*."

We're frozen, statues cursed to hear the rest of this story. The Great Hall is eerie in its red-painted quiet.

Outside, the sun's almost gone. Darkness creeps in around us; it feels like the whole world shrinks down to the eight of us at this fold-out table. It's just us and the story. The *history*—Nostrils swears this really happened.

My breath catches in my throat. Anticipation tingles up and down my spine. My stomach balls itself into a tight fist, along with my heart. Finally, I manage to whisper, "What's in the lake, Nostrils?"

"Vampire devils!"

Suddenly, a banshee screams!

The bloody sound cuts like steel. It slices through my skull and drives into my brain. Long, clawed fingers dig into my ribs. They're going to plunge through the skin. They'll peel the bones apart with a snap! They're going to tear out my heart and my lungs right in front of me! I'll be alive and watch myself die, bit by bit.

I snap and scream too, throwing my arms up to try to protect myself.

And then I'm confused, because everyone's laughing.

Lowering my arms, I hear the echo of the screams in my ears. They turn into words. Words spoken by familiar voices. Ew did the screaming, and Bowl Cut did the grabbing.

They got me. They pulled a stupid prank, and they totally got me.

Nostrils laughs. "Two-hearted vampire devils who drink your blood and steal your soul! They live in the lake. They're coming for youuuuuuu!"

My heart pounds and I feel dizzy. It was just a stupid ghost story, just like Corryn's golden arm bit. And I *fell* for it. Again! Everybody's laughing at me, wondering out loud if I peed my pants. The spike of adrenaline makes me sick to my stomach, but I remember what my dad said before I left. *Sometimes, you have to play along to get along, Tez.*

Even though my face is hot and my chest feels like it's going to burst, I plaster on a smile. I laugh.

"Good one, guys," I concede gamely.

After everybody has their turn imitating me screaming, the conversation moves on.

I should have realized I wasn't actually dying. My life didn't even flash before my eyes, which honestly had felt vaguely disappointing in the midst of all the terror. Wilted, I open my bag of carrot sticks and just stare at them. I don't feel like eating right now. I feel dumb and exposed, and also uncomfortable.

Corryn's the only one who notices I'm not talking. She leans over and whispers, "That was kind of mean. You want me to sock somebody for you?"

I don't. But the offer soothes me. She's probably never played along to get along in her entire life. When I smile this time, for her, it's real. "I'll let you know."

Rubbing her fist like she's polishing it, Corryn says, "Anytime, Tez."

Tez. My real name. Not Chickenlips.

Well, how about that?

I think we might be friends.

4
Faces in the Fire

Tez

The bonfire was aflame to a degree that my dad would call "fair to middling."

Big, but not ancient-druid kind of big. Nowhere near big enough to upset any anthropomorphic bears with forest ranger credentials. It's disappointing, honestly.

Everybody but me is bouncing around like pachinko balls, amped up on nighttime and hot dogs—even Corryn.

The thing is, there are issues with the fire. I raise my voice to point it out. "See, the problem is that we're burning birch. Birch burns hot, but it goes up really fast! Do we have any maple?"

Exactly zero people answer my question. Our huge pile of firewood is almost gone, and I'm not allowed to inspect it for better logs. That was the first thing Gavin told me, and now he stands by the pile like a bulldog. A bulldog with a British accent and a knack for picking the wettest, moldiest branches to toss onto the bonfire.

When he does, a fug of nasty greenish smoke washes over us. Most of the girls scatter upwind, shrieking.

"I dare you to breathe it," Nostrils shouts. Two seconds later, Knees and Bowl Cut are gagging and retching. Across the fire, Ew lives up to her name, over and over and over. As in, "Ohmigod, you guys! Ew!"

Corryn drifts over and stands sort of near me. We're in a good, medium spot. Not too much smoke, but plenty of warmth. The heat from the too-hot birch makes Corryn's brown hair float up a little. Her cheeks are red, and she waves a wobbly hot dog in my general direction.

"Do you know a lot about trees?" she asks.

I smile at her and nod. "I studied all aspects of camping before we got here. I wanted to make sure I did it right."

"Must be nice," Corryn says. "I didn't even know I was coming until the last minute."

Wow, surprise camp? That sounds scary. My parents have never sprung anything on me last minute, not in my entire life. I'm not sure how I would feel about that. Exhilarated? Terrified? Exhilified?

I ask, "You don't want to be here?"

She stares into the fire instead of looking at me. "They sent me away so they can get a divorce in peace. I mean, whatever, right? Double birthdays and double Christmases for me. Whoopie."

"Oh wow," I say. I pat her shoulder awkwardly. "I'm—really sorry."

Impaling another hot dog on a stick, Corryn says, "Who cares? Anyway, you can identify wood and stuff, right?"

"Absolutely," I say. She wants to change the subject, therefore, we're changing the subject.

"I read about the native plants of Ohio, and wilderness survival, and shelter construction, and more. Not only can I identify wood, I'm pretty sure I can build a log cabin, make a working bow and set of arrows, and smoke a whole wild hog. Obviously, we would have to catch the hog first."

Corryn thrusts her hot dog into the flames. Right

into them, deep into the core. Like, practically up to her wrist.

"If you're not careful, you're going to set it on fire."

Smoke drifts around us, and she pulls her stick free. She holds it up like Excalibur—a flaming, blistering Excalibur.

She tells me, "It's not good if it's not burnt."

There are two kinds of people in the world: the burners and the toasters. I look around at everyone in Oak Camp and realize there are only two toasters—me and Ew. That might be a bad thing. I may need to reconsider my stance.

Corryn waves the stick until her weenie fire goes out. Then she bites at the scorched bubbles with relish. "All right, wood," she says, looking at me expectantly. "I found a big, gnarly log on our nature walk. It was black and . . . gnarly. What is it?"

That wasn't a lot to go on. Squinting at her, I ask, "What kind of bark did it have? Was it smooth or rough?"

Corryn shrugs. "Smooth, I guess. It was cold. And heavy."

"Did it smell like anything?"

With that, Corryn takes a half step back from me. She looks me over with annoyance, then shakes her head. "Never mind."

"I'm not messing with you. That's a serious question!"

"I'm not a *wood sniffer*," she says. She seems both offended and like she's holding out. Like she wants to say something else but is afraid to ask me any more questions. Mostly because the next one could be, What did it taste like? I don't say anything. I'm not going to accidentally call her a wood licker too.

"Right, you box of knobs," Gavin shouts. "Last of the wood; finish the wieners and marshmallows, or get out of our faces and go to bed!"

A happy chorus echoes in our camp. Flaming sugar before bed! Everybody's hyped, but Corryn grabs my arm. Hard. She spins me to look at Gavin and gives me a shake. "That kind! That! What's that?"

Gavin tosses a strange, twisted branch into the fire.

She described it perfectly, and I shudder as it rolls and settles into the flames. Suddenly queasy, I still do my best to identify it. There's a soft hiss that rises to a whistle. Then the branch pops. It spits embers into the air, and this time, everybody squeals.

"It's the vampire devils!" Ew exclaims.

The wood snaps and belches up some pale gray smoke. Bluish flames lick over the log, like they're trying to find a way inside.

"It must be wet," I say. That's the only explanation for the popping and spitting and blue fire. I'm about to diagnose it as belonging to spruce or pine, but then it screams.

The wood *screams*!

The sound shrieks out. It tears across the lake and drains all the heat from my skin. It's a sound so deep and terrible, it feels like it has clutching, grabbing claws.

When the scream dies, everybody but Corryn and me laughs. I sit down hard on my stump-chair.

That wasn't the sound of wet wood making funny noises. It was something alive . . . and terrified.

It screams again: human sounds, wrenched from throats and tongues and teeth. It's like kids screaming, and not from joy. This is terror; petrified souls howling into the night.

I probably only think that because, I swear to Darth Vader, I see something in the smoke and swirl of the blue fire.

In the heart of the fire, in the hottest part of it,

three floating faces rise from the embers. They look old-fashioned, with funny hairdos and high-necked collars. For a second, it's like a daguerreotype photo in flames.

They're so real, so present, that I reach toward them.

The heat bites my fingers; I jerk my hand back.

It was the wrong thing to do. It's like I angered something, reaching for them. It's like I set off something evil.

The screaming rises again. The faces change.

To skulls.

Only skulls. Mouths wide open. Dark sockets staring back at us.

The scream dies, and suddenly, it's silent as the grave.

According to the *Camper's Guidebook*, there's always supposed to be a counselor on duty.

That's probably why Gavin threatened to gut us if we told anybody when he snuck out a moment ago.

No chaperone means no showers for our cabin tonight. That's both a good and a bad thing. We won't have to hike half a mile down the path with flashlights to get to the showers. But we hiked all day, then baked in the stink of sweat and smoke at the bonfire.

The bonfire—which I am desperately trying to forget.

This is a problem, because the cabin is narrow and small, and smells like hundred-year-old wood. (And the four of us smell like summer sausage.) The bunks are built in and the windows have these shutters that barely open. We have a box fan for ventilation. All it does is spread our stench around.

We get ready for bed in our own personal ways.

Me? I'm writing notes in my field journal about the bad stick that turned the fire into a horror movie. If I write it down on the page, I'll have a better chance of getting it out of my head. I'd be more scared, but the lights are on.

Knees throws himself on his bunk. Not to sleep—to kick the mattress above him. It's just a thin, plastic-covered pad, and every time he kicks it, it wheezes. Kick, *whuup*, kick, *whuup*. It's hard to concentrate on dread evil with that going on.

Bowl Cut strips down to his underpants and sits in front of the box fan. His skin is incandescently white.

It's almost blue; I can practically see his veins between his millions of freckles. He has a lot of confidence, displaying himself this way. It's probably a side effect of his legendary haircut.

Turning to point the fan at Nostrils, Bowl Cut asks, "So, what are you?"

Looking to me, Nostrils rolls his eyes but answers. "Korean. But I was born in Philadelphia. Before you start, Godzilla is Japanese, egg rolls are Chinese, and you don't know anything Korean but me."

That's the best answer I've ever heard for that question. I give Nostrils two thumbs-up and say, "Kimchi and yubu chobap."

"You know cho—"

"Chickenlips!" Curiosity only stretches so far for Bowl Cut. He turns the fan toward me. "What are you?"

In the future, I'll probably steal Nostrils' answer. But since he's sitting right there, I say what I always say. "My mom is from Indiana. My dad is from Guam."

Bowl Cut digests this. "Then you're Guamanian."

"No," I say. "I'm *half* Chamorro."

"Whatever, Guamanian," Bowl Cut replies. Then he turns the fan to Knees. "Hey! What are you?"

Baffled, Knees shrugs. "I don't know. Generic American black dude?"

"Me too," Bowl Cut says. "I mean, American white dude. But yeah."

Everybody goes quiet, so I guess the census is done. That means the floor is open for new business. Abandoning my field journal, I stand up in the middle of the cabin. "Okay, show of hands. Who saw three screaming skulls in the fire?"

I raise my hand. Knees replies with a pillow to my gut.

"Don't even try that," he warns. "I'm not scared of vampire devils, and I'm not scared of fire."

Quickly, I try to clarify. "I'm not afraid of fire either. I was disconcerted by the *faces* in the fire. There were three of them. All scary and *gahhhhhhhh*." I pull my fingers down my face and roll my eyes around; it's the best impersonation of screaming fire ghosts that I've got in my arsenal.

Knees frowns at me. "That's not cool, man. It's gonna be lights-out soon."

Through the fan, Bowl Cut repeats, his voice wavering through the blades. "Thaaaat's not coooool maaaaan! Thaaat's disconcerrrrrted!"

"Okay, one, that should be disconcert*ing*," I say. "And two, I'm not trying to scare anybody. I'm asking a legitimate question. Did you see it? Or not?"

"Nobody saw anything in the fire, Chickenlips." Nostrils shakes his head at me. Like he's disappointed. I wonder for a second if he thought I was cool.

Bowl Cut stands up. "I saw something in the fire!"

Hopeful, I ask, "What?"

Whipping around, Bowl Cut pulls down his tighty-whities and presses his very pale butt to the fan. Then he farts. The fan chops the sound to bits, and Knees and Nostrils scream with laughter. I have a feeling I'm going to be hearing that a lot this summer.

I open our door to let in some air. Across the path, the lights are still on in the girls' cabin. I wonder if Corryn's still awake. I think she saw the faces. At least, I hope she did.

Otherwise, I might be going crazy on the first day of camp.

5
A Delicate Condition

June 7, 1983

Corryn

Ew steps up on her bunk and shakes me.

"Breakfast," she says when I blink at her in confusion.

I have no memory of sleep. I must have drifted off sometime in there, but it feels like I didn't even close my eyes. The sun is shining like it's ready to go to war. Settle down, sun.

The first thing I hear is a baffling *shoooosh* noise. It sounds like a hot air balloon is taking off in our cabin. I look over and see it is actually Hairspray spraying an enormous can of hairspray into her hair. *Shooooosh shooosh shoosh.* I think she really did bring a case of Aqua Net. To camp.

I yawn and stretch and pretend like it was a normal night. I pretend like I had a quiet night of peaceful slumber and not an awful waking nightmare. I roll over and look at the poster of Danny Stark I tacked up next to my bed. Not even his smile (or the fact that he's doing a sick power wheelie) can shake the gloom.

"Good morning, You!" Scary Mary says. She's standing in the middle of the cabin brushing her teeth. I wonder what she's going to do when it's time to spit.

"My name is Corryn," I say.

"And my name is I-DON'T-CARE," she says. Nice. "In fact, if anyone uses civilian names in this cabin, that will be a one bead deduction. Got it?" Toothpaste foams at the corners of her big old mouth. Rabidly, she rattles a jar with a few purple and orange spheres in it.

I vaguely recall the *Camper's Guidebook* mentioning a system of beads but I didn't think much of it. Are we really supposed to care about this?

"Don't cost us beads!" Hairspray and Braids say in unison. Then they yell "jinx!" and then fall over dying from laughter.

Oooookay then. Guess some of us care.

I grab my bug spray (things with lots of legs lurk inside camp toilets) and start down the path without a word.

"Bolt down that breakfast, and then arts and crafts straight after, You!" Scary Mary yells. "Don't be late!"

Breakfast is damp scrambled eggs and sad bacon. It takes a lot of work to ruin bacon, so I'm glad when it's time to head to arts and crafts. I'm not artistic or anything. I just want to get away from the tragedy on my plate.

Except, it turns out, arts and crafts is held in a rotten building. Literally rotten.

Someone recently painted the walls, but the mottled color doesn't do much to cover decaying wood. The floor has been patched in a lot of places but it still looks like there is a good chance of falling through if you jump. Maybe just if you walk too heavily. It's definitely seen better days.

This whole camp looks like it's seen better days.

Mom and Dad both told me tons of stories about how much they loved their summer camp in New Hampshire when they were little. It's actually where they met.

They were both counselors there in the sixties too. While they were there, Dad made Mom a macramé pennant with "Friends Forever" spelled out in beads.

Ha. Turns out even stupid fiber crafts lie.

Could I meet *my* future ex-husband here? It seems unlikely. I look around at the grody boys farting on each other and shouting insulting nicknames. It seems insane. Who will be the future former Mr. Corryn Quinn? Knees? Bowl Cut? (He really does have pretty nice hair.) The Korean guy whose name I don't know? Or maybe Tez?

You know what? Forget about it. These squabs can't touch me. I go back to my original summer survival plan: counting the money for Elliot's mag wheels, five bucks at a time.

Tez is the only one from Oak Camp already working on his lanyard. He didn't need to wait for instruction. He weaves the plastic laces at an impressive pace. His nimble fingers have turned out two key chains already, before anyone else has even started. He doesn't look happy though. His bright eyes are encircled by dark rings.

I try to watch his technique, though my heart isn't

really in this. There are lots of other arts and crafts supplies sitting in bins on the tables. I like drawing, so I grab a few markers and a pad of paper. I realize that Scary Mary might yell at me for straying from the assignment. I might even cost our cabin a bead. What a horror!

My favorite thing to draw is Elliot. I can trace the shape of his wheels and the line of his frame from memory. I can draw a pretty good Danny Stark too. I start in, but for some reason, the markers don't want to move in this way. I guess I'm still thinking about the bonfire last night, because all I can draw is one thing.

Well, three things.

Three faces screaming. Three faces with their eyes, hair, and mouths full of flames. I hate looking at them, but I can't stop drawing them. The faces fill the page, their eyes boring into me. The fire fills the top half of the sheet and the bottom half of the page fills with the drip, drip, drip of pouring blood.

I feel a scary presence looming behind me. A Scary Mary presence.

"Wotcher doing there, You?" she says. "That's one dodgy lanyard."

I quickly fold up the paper and try to hide it in my lap.

"You too, Chickenlips!" Mary says.

You know what? Now that I think about it, I'm lucky I'm just "You." Chickens don't even have lips. But then, I don't think Gavin's exactly swimming around in extra brains.

But why is Mary scolding Tez? He's been doing nothing but making lanyard after lanyard like some sort of robot . . . that . . . makes lanyards.

I look over and realize that, at some point, Tez stopped weaving. Like me, he has a piece of paper and a red marker in his hand. There is a far-off look in his eyes. His hand moves automatically, drawing so hard that the markers squeak on the paper.

I can't see exactly what he's drawing, but if I had three guesses, all three would be faces in a fire.

He snaps out of his trance when Mary flicks him in the back of the head. Dazed, he crumples up the drawing. He shoves it in his sock.

"Oh, you're the weird one, then, Chickenlips," she says. "They told me there'd be one."

There is something weird here, but it's not Tez.

And I think we need to figure out exactly what it is.

Tez

After arts and crafts, we split off and head to the sports we signed up for before camp.

At least, everybody else does.

As for me, I watch Corryn and the rest pack up and leave. Then, when I'm sure none of them can see me, I make the short walk to the front of camp. Passing the Recreation Barn, I squint when I hear strange, jangly music spilling from its windows. Somebody, somewhere in this camp, is square dancing today. I hope it's not me.

The trees part from the path and sunlight spills down. On the right is the big parking lot and staff cabins, but to my right is the whole place laid out. Tennis courts and basketball courts, a big lawn for frisbee and soccer. Past that, on the lake, kids shriek as they jump in for the first time.

It's not super-hot yet, so I bet Lake Sweetwater is more like Lake Icewater. I'm not looking forward to getting into it. If I'm lucky, the bright sun will warm it up before my swim test. (For the record, that's basically delusional thinking. In a direct battle between the volume of water versus the available energy from the sun, volume wins every time. It'll be blue skin and chattering teeth as far as the eye can see.)

When I reach the Great Hall, I consider my options. The infirmary is right there, but I think I'm supposed to talk to the director. She's probably not in the canteen, although a shockingly chipper blonde is, arranging cherry Jolly Ranchers next to the candy cigarettes and Blow Pops.

There doesn't seem to be anyone in the open Great Hall, so that leaves the camp office. I knock, then look up when Mrs. Winchelhauser opens the door. At first, she stares at me suspiciously. Then a spark of recognition lights the eyes behind her unusual glasses.

"Oh! You must be . . ."

"Tez," I say before she tries to pronounce my first name. "Tez Jones."

Mrs. Winchelhauser smiles and opens the door a little wider. "Yes, of course, come in."

Stepping inside, I'm not sure where I'm supposed to be exactly. Stacks of papers tower out of control on every available surface. Two file cabinets stand sentinel by the door, and half their drawers are open. On top of the file cabinets there's a microphone for the PA system, and a brass bell with a wooden handle—presumably the very instrument that Mrs. Winchelhauser uses over the aforementioned PA system to signal the end of an activity period.

The nameplate on her desk is upside down, and the huge camp map on the wall hangs so precariously that it might succumb to gravity at any moment.

I'd say it looks like Mrs. Winchelhauser is trying to rob the place, but I don't see anything to steal.

"I'm sorry," Mrs. Winchelhauser says, "I'm still trying to get organized for the summer."

The door opens behind me, bumping my shoulder blade. I look back, and at the same time, Mrs. Winchelhauser exclaims, "Oh good, there you are."

"You" is a woman in khakis and a nurse's shirt. The shirt has hundreds of tiny stethoscopes printed all over it. Her name tag has the Camp Sweetwater logo, but nothing else—no name.

Plucking a label maker from the desk, Mrs. Winchelhauser hands it to the woman. "I wasn't sure how to spell it."

I look at her sympathetically as she starts to tick it out. Nobody knows how to spell—or say—my name either.

Archimedes Tesla Jones.

Special, right?

Instead of eating the hearts of their enemies to gain their strengths like the Celts did, my parents stole the names of their idols and gave them to their kids. They said the goal was to imbue us with their spirit and curiosity. Instead, it guarantees we'll never, ever find a pencil or a bike license plate with our names printed on it. (My four-year-old sister is named Hypatia Marie. We call her "Hi.")

"This is Miss Kortepeter," Mrs. Winchelhauser says, clearing an edge of her desk to lean on. A book tips off the corner and plops into the trash can, but Mrs. Winchelhauser ignores it. "Miss Kortepeter is the camp nurse, and she's been explaining your condition to me."

"Marfan," I confirm, then add, "loose joint syndrome. Did you know that Abraham Lincoln probably had it too? There's no way to be sure; it wasn't identified as a condition until 1896. President Lincoln enjoyed his last half play in 1865."

Mrs. Winchelhauser looks at me blankly. "Fascinating. But as I was saying, Miss Kortepeter has filled me in, and I read the letter your parents sent—very helpful. When you write home, please thank them for me."

"You bet," I say.

"Yes, all right, what was I saying? Oh yes," Mrs. Winchelhauser says. "Given your delicate condition—"

With a frown, I say, "I'm not delicate. I just can't do stuff that pumps up my heart rate, or hits me right in the chest. Baseball, football, wrestling . . . bullfighting is probably out, but I didn't see that on the camp activities list."

Ha *ha*? My joke does a little death spiral, punctuated by the *ker-chik!* of Miss Kortepeter cutting the plastic label from the roll. She peels the tape off and plasters her name on her tag. "No rock climbing, horseback riding, soccer . . ."

All of this is stuff I know. I had to *beg* to come to camp, and part of begging was identifying for my parents every part of camp that might explode my potentially weak heart, and then promising them that I would avoid those parts completely. (PS, I'm pretty sure that horseback riding isn't *that* exciting.)

Marfan syndrome has its perks: my joints are so loose I can bend all of them backward (an excellent party trick, or so I hear; still waiting to be invited to a party) and I'm probably going to be wicked tall. Good chance I'll look great in a stovepipe hat.

It also has its issues: my aorta could split with a

stiff breeze. No big. Twelve-year-olds drop dead from heart attacks all the time! I could even die falling out of bed.

That one bothers my mom, but not me. Statistically, *anybody* could die falling out of a bed. It's the most common way to die in your own house! You could also kick it by falling out of a tub. Or off a chair. Your home is a deathtrap! But we don't spend all day safely lying on the floor!

I'm *ready* to actually do some stuff (not dying; I can definitely wait for that adventure). Camp Sweetwater had promised I could have a "modified," meaning non-fatal, schedule.

Which was sort of what I was waiting to hear. Prompting Mrs. Winchelhauser, I say, "So instead of sports stuff . . ."

Mrs. Winchelhauser smiles. "We thought you might enjoy helping out with some of the younger campers in arts and crafts until things like the photography lab and camp radio station are set up. We're hoping to have them open soon."

I blink. "You want me to work . . . with little kids."

"Unless you had a better idea?"

Well, I knew I didn't want to collect more wood.

Starting haunted fires wasn't high on my list of experiences to revisit. Definitely didn't want to investigate the source of every known bug in Ohio turning up in Oak Camp Cabin Group C, so . . .

Flashing her my best impress-an-adult smile, I say, "Nope, that sounds great! When do I start?"

"Right after your swim test," Mrs. Winchelhauser says. But then she looks to Miss Kortepeter. "Can he swim?"

Miss Kortepeter straightens her name tag. "No high dives, no belly flops, no chicken."

"No problem," I say, and slip away.

Long as I can keep my adventures with the kidlets in Bantam Camp under wraps, it'll be no problem at all.

6
Swim Test of the Danged

Tez

The swim test isn't supposed to be fun. And that's good, because it isn't.

There are a million kids at the lakeshore, and as previously mentioned, Ohio decided to give us something like a fresh March day in the middle of June. Dark nimbostratus clouds sink over the far side of the lake, gusting a cold wind in our direction.

A bunch of the girls huddle together under their towels. Smart—they're sharing body heat. If there's an apocalypse, they're the ones who are going to survive.

"Hiii-yah!" Knees shouts and kicks at my face. I don't flinch. It's not because I have nerves of steel. It's because this is the sixth time he's done it. We're allowed to kung fu each other as long as nobody touches.

This rule came from Gavin, who didn't want to hear that *hi-ya* is a bastardization of traditional karate breath flow and has nothing to do with kung fu. He did dock our cabin one bead because he didn't understand that bastardization isn't a curse word. (Since I'm not supposed to participate in heart-exploding activities, I mostly watch, and try not to flinch.)

Knees whirls around. I think he's trying for a flying spin kick. Instead, he face-plants and Bowl Cut laughs so hard he blows a snot bubble. Yep. When the apocalypse comes, the girls are definitely going to be the ones to survive.

The lifeguards blow the whistles. The sound goes straight into my brain. It makes me shiver and I don't know why.

"Line up!" the lifeguards shout.

As soon as they take charge, Mary bolts. She'd said something about heading into the woods for some herbs. I hope she knows her field guide. There's a lot of super-poisonous hemlock in the woods around Camp Sweetwater, and it looks just like wild carrots.

I hurry to get in line. I already know how to swim,

and also, I'm good at tests. I listen to all the instructions. Then I ask questions if I don't understand anything. Mom says lots of people are too shy to speak up, so if I do, I'm really helping everybody. Sometimes, I even ask questions when I already know the answer, to help the rest of the class.

Corryn ends up right behind me, wearing her orange-and-green-striped towel like a cape. She doesn't recognize me at first. Probably because I wrapped my towel into a perfect turban. I wave a hand in front of her face. "Hey."

Startled, Corryn looks at me hard. Then she looks around. "All right," she says. But then she doesn't say anything else. I wonder if she's thinking about her mom and dad. I've been thinking about mine a lot. And I'm lucky. I know they're both going to be there when I get home.

"The first test," the lifeguard shouts, "will be a sixty-second float."

"What are we going to do?" Corryn asks.

I look to the lifeguard, then back at her. She's not paying attention; I can't blame her. Quietly, I tell her, "A sixty-second float."

With a roll of her eyes, Corryn pushes a finger into

my ribs. Hard. "Not about the swim test, duh. About the faces."

The wind shifts again, and my whole body prickles with the cold. Wrapping my arms around myself, I try to split myself into two. One ear listening to the lifeguard, one ear listening to Corryn. This is not an efficient use of my senses, but I try anyway.

"Nothing," I say. "I mean. We won't gather firewood from anything black and gnarly from here on out."

The lifeguard blows his whistle. "When you hear that, you know what to do."

Wait, what?! Panic rises in my chest. I don't know what to do! But before I can raise my hand and ask, Corryn catches my wrist. She shakes my hand around, emphatic.

"What if it wasn't the wood? What if there's something freaky going on here?"

"Dead man's float," the lifeguard chimes in helpfully.

Now it feels like something freaky is going on for sure. The wind kicks little white waves up on the lake. The dark clouds drift toward us, and what's weird is that in some places, it's super sunny. But in others, it's really dark. I don't know why, but now I don't want to get in the water, like at all.

Swallowing hard, I hunch my shoulders up and shake my head. "It's just one thing. And yes, it was scary. But it's just one thing. We don't have enough data to decide there's overall freakiness going on."

"Tez. In arts and crafts, we were drawing the same thing. And neither one of us could stop!"

My guts kind of flop over, and I break out in a queasy sweat. My mouth is all sour, warning me that barf could happen anytime. Gathering up a bunch of spit in my mouth, I swallow it all at once. I say, reasonably, "We were drawing the same thing because we saw the same thing. We had counselors breathing down our necks; of course we couldn't stop. Coincidences aren't causation."

"Okay, fine! What about the bug flood?"

"We're outside," I say reasonably. "The outside is full of bugs."

Corryn huffs at me; her breath smells like Juicy Fruit gum. "I can't believe you're going chicken on me."

Before I can reply, Knees yells, "HIII-YAH," and lands his very first high kick.

In the middle of my face.

I go down hard, the salty taste of blood in the back of

my throat before I even land. My chest feels remarkably calm. This heart isn't ready to say goodbye. However, my guts decide that now is definitely the time to say hello.

All the girls around me scream and scatter when I puke. Chunky scrambled eggs, orange juice, and red, red, red from my nosebleed.

I'm thinking, if they can't handle a little barf, they might not survive the apocalypse after all.

Corryn

"Oh brilliant, Chickenlips chundered all up and down the dock. Lovely, just lovely, Chickenlips."

Gavin is really not pleased about this.

"Um, Knees kicked him in the face," I try to explain, but Gavin rushes past me, arms flailing and British swears flying.

I guess "chundered" means threw up and "lovely" means not lovely. "Brilliant" also means not brilliant. Some of the other words he yells I don't have any idea about. All I know is that he drags Tez out of his bloody chunder puddle and marches him toward the infirmary.

The lifeguard guy isn't fazed at all. He is very tan and very wrinkly, like a human walnut. With a handlebar mustache. He's also wearing a tank top that I *think* is sewed to his trunks.

He's also seriously old. He's supposed to guard our lives, but what I want to know is, who's guarding *him* from the grim reaper?

"You're next," he says, stroking his mustache. I just stare at him.

"Get floating!" He grabs me by the arm. Old Lifeguard is sinewy and strong. His grasp is hard, his hands rough. I slide across the slick dock and can't hit the brakes. I tumble gracelessly into the lake. I hope my parents feel really guilty if this guy gets me killed.

The water bites with a fierce cold against my skin. I sink deep into the green water. Deep and deeper still, tasting muck and algae. I had my towel around my shoulders, so it follows me into the water. It looks like a jellyfish or terry-cloth sea creature from the great beyond.

I try to get my bearings and position my body into proper float pose. It's not fair! I didn't even have time to take a deep breath. The towel is tangled around my legs. I kick it to get it free.

That's when I feel it. It's moving—all on its own. Slithering. Writhing like a moray eel. It *tangles* around my legs, on *purpose*.

No. No, no, no!

I kick and kick again, but the harder I do, the tighter the towel knots. As I struggle, I sink. Oh, God. I'm going to drown!

I spin around and claw at my feet. I figure I have a few seconds to free myself before I pass out.

Beneath me, the water . . . changes. That's the only word for it. It boils with a sick, green glow.

Every time I get my fingers into the loop of the towel, they slip out. White-hot shocks of pain streak up as my nails bend backward.

My brain explodes with stars. It's like a headache in color. In my ears, my pulse beats out SOS, over and over. Something like thunder rocks through the water. My bones rattle. My lungs burn in a thousand tiny pin-pricks. They're dying—

I'm dying.

Thrashing, I fight to free myself. But I've been down here so long. How long? I don't even know. One Mississippi, two Mississippi . . . . I'm going to sink to the bottom where the vampire devils live and never be seen again. Three Mississippi, ten Missouris, sixteen Pennsylvanias . . .

It's getting dark, and I'm getting tired. Even my brain is tired, thinking slowly. My mind wanders: instead of screaming at me to fight, it drifts into daydreams. I knew Old Lifeguard was a bust. He's probably standing up there stroking his mustache and thinking about bran muffins.

NO! Get with it, Corryn! This is not how you go out! Not here! Not today!

With all my air bubbling out of my mouth, I grab at the towel again.

It's gone!

I'm free! My body snaps like a rubber band. I shoot back up to the surface. Forget about passing the test, I just want to live!

As soon as I spring up above the water, I gobble up deep breaths. The cold air slaps me in the face, and I'm good with that. Slap away, sweet, sweet breathable oxygen. Slap away!

Treading water, I look around. Right next to me, my towel floats on the waves. I know it's mine—bright orange-and-green stripes. QUINN is no doubt scribbled on the corner. But it makes no sense. My towel can't be bobbing on the surface next to me. It was just deep under the water, winding itself around my ankles.

Or, *something* was.

I dive back under, desperate to see it. If it wasn't my towel grabbing at my ankles, what was it?

What kind of wild animals live in this lake? Giant squid? An angry octopus? Seaweed? This isn't the sea! It doesn't make any sense.

I swim deeper and see . . . nothing. I do, however, hear something. At first, it's a whine—it comes at a distance, shrill and unnerving. The green glow is no longer, but this sound bubbles up from the deep. It's not a whistle, it's not a whine anymore—

It's screaming.

Not from the campers on the dock. No, there's no playfulness in this. It's the ragged, raspy cry of terror. Of hauntings.

It's the screaming that came from the fire, and it pierces me like icy needles.

What's worse is that behind the screaming, I hear something else. Something worse.

Laughter. Deep and rumbling.

Something grabs me under the arms and I kick and claw and punch. I burst through the surface, still fighting.

"What the . . . ?!" the voice asks. It is not a sea monster. It's the Old Lifeguard. Where the heck was he a couple of Mississippis ago when I was actually drowning?!

"Settle down, girl!" He pulls me into shallower water, then roughly drags me onto the shore. He puts a hand to his lip like he expects to see blood.

"I was fine," I yell. Scrambling to my feet, I drip rivers onto the gravelly sand. The Old Lifeguard hands me a towel, since mine has sunk down into the lake. I look toward the water and shudder. Don't tell *me* to settle down. I was trying to save my life!

Scrubbing my face with the towel, I tell him, "There's something in the water."

For a moment, the Old Lifeguard stares at me. It's almost like he recognizes me from somewhere else. But then his face goes blank, and he moves on to the next kid. When I drop the towel, I look for Tez in the crowd of people on the shore, but he's gone. Still at the infirmary, probably. That means I'm totally alone.

A female lifeguard stands at the end of the dock, urging one of the little girls into the water.

I can't look when she jumps in.

I can only wait for the sound of her scream.

7
Drip Drip Drip

Tez

The backs of my thighs feel like overrun ant hills, prickly and poky and itchy.

The sheets on this infirmary bed are scratchy, but at least I'm inside. It's slightly warmer in here. It smells like iodine and lemon, ammonia and bleach. Sort of hospitaly, and Miss Kortepeter has really soft hands.

"Were you unconscious at all?" she asks as she pumps up the blood pressure cuff again.

I shake my head. "No."

"Did you have breakfast?"

"Yes, lots," I say. I don't share that I feel like I threw

up about a third more than I ate. It's probably not relevant. Or, strictly speaking, scientifically possible. Even though the infirmary is far away from the lake, and inside, and warm, I don't really want to spend nine weeks of camp here. I've spent enough time in hospitals, thanks.

She lets the air out of the cuff (to be absolutely correct, it's called a sphygmomanometer) and then peels it off my arm. Her soft hands tip my head back, then forward. I don't know what she's looking for. If she wants to see some loose joint action, I can dislocate my shoulder for her. My head usually stays right where it belongs, though.

Finally, she *hmphs*.

"Nothing looks broken. You might have a black eye coming in, though. Go ahead and lie down. I'll get you an ice pack. Try not to fall asleep."

Sprawling back, I stare at the ceiling. The infirmary, like the Great Hall and the cabins, is made from big beams of wood. They make patterns on the ceiling, stretching toward the peak of the roof.

I trace them with my eyes, but it makes me drowsy. No! Can't fall asleep!

Still, heavy, heavy, the sleepiness pulls me down; it's an anchor attached to the middle of my chest, drawing me deep into the mattress.

The angles of the walls shift. It's subtle at first. The shadows don't line up. One of the light fixtures hangs at an impossible angle. Maybe I do have a concussion? I rub my head and open my eyes wide. I *focus.*

Suddenly, the outside wall, with all the windows, seems much taller than the rest. It just stretches way up. I expect the sound of creaking timber as it moves like elastic, but there's only silence, and the sound of my heart skipping beats.

A little dizzy, I grab the sides of the cot and blink hard. Anytime now, the room should go back to its normal shape. Annnny time now.

Instead, the ceiling staggers into the distance, then drops really close to my face, a rubber band snapped back to its normal shape. It blurs—no, my *vision* blurs. It has to be my vision, because buildings don't just rearrange themselves. But I feel like I'm underwater, slow and sinking back into the bed, down into the depths.

Shadows gather and stretch. They make strange, monstrous shapes that creep up the walls. They have long heads, long claws, long arms stretching out for me. My stomach turns and I close my eyes.

Knees must have kicked me harder than I realized. But unless he broke my nose and sent a shard of bone into my brain (unlikely) or detached my retina (slightly more likely), the kick has nothing to do with everything looking weird.

It's just . . . it sounds crazy, but I feel like I can *feel* the lake behind me. Like it's dark, kind of alive, and . . . reaching for me.

The nurse must have gone to the Great Hall to get the ice pack, but I don't think I'm alone in here. Those shadows on the walls loom. I don't want to look. I make myself look. They're still here. They're everywhere.

I hear something from the other side of the curtain. At first, it's slow and steady—as if someone didn't turn the sink tap quite tight enough. But it gets faster, a steady, trickling beat.

Drip. Drip. Drip.

The roof could be leaking. Is it raining?

I twist to look outside. The sky is angry and dark, and a wind whips through the trees. But I don't see any rain. And the sound is coming from inside the infirmary. Maybe a pipe burst? Or maybe—my brain trails off. There aren't that many things that go drip-drip-drip in the world.

Even though I feel really heavy, I stand up. I shuffle like there are invisible chains around my ankles. Each step I take goes on forever. The air is thick, like molasses, like tar. The fabric divider isn't that big, but I'm moving in slow motion. It takes almost a million years to get to it. The walls keep changing height, the ceiling stretching up and lunging down so low I want to duck.

Drip. Drip. Drip.

The sound echoes in a weird way. As though the small infirmary is a tunnel now, one that goes on and on into the distance.

The sound quickens.

Drip-drip-drip.

"Miss Kortepeter?" I call. My stomach tightens. My head is suddenly too full. I take one more leaden step and push the divider open.

The nurse stands in front of the sink, frighteningly still. She hunches over it, her shoulder blades so sharp they look like broken wings. And that's not all that's wrong with her. Her hair is loose and wet. It hangs heavily around her head. Dark, wet beads slip from her hair onto the floor, all the way around her.

Drip-drip-drip-drip-drip.

The drops puddle on the floor around her feet, forming a dark lake. Too dark to be water. It's *not* water. It's deep red. It's—

I manage to make a helpless sound. It's not the scream I wanted, but that's all that comes out. Even if I did scream, who would hear me? Everyone else is at the lake.

There's no one here to help me. No one here but her.

Woozy, I reach for something to steady myself. I can't scream and now I can't run away. This is daytime. It's not night; and yet, I'm exhausted. My head hurts, but headaches don't do this.

Something is wrong. Something is wrong with *this place.*

Corryn was right. She was right and I blew her off and . . .

DRIP.

Everything snaps back into place. The light comes back on, the walls are even, the ceiling is at a reasonable angle.

"Tez!" Miss Kortepeter exclaims as she comes through the front door.

Her hair is twisted into a bouncy ponytail. She's

dry and looks really confused. My insides turn to liquid when I look to the sink.

No one there.

Nothing on the floor.

The sound has stopped and my knees give up.

"Blood," I say, and wobble.

She rushes over to me. "Did your nose start bleeding again? Come on, let's get you comfortable."

In a flurry of motion, Miss Kortepeter gets me back to the cot and settled on the thin pillow. She carefully arranges the cold pack on my face and tells me to try to relax.

Relax. *Right.*

I heard something. I saw *something.* Faces in the fire, and now blood in the infirmary. There's something going on at Camp Sweetwater, and it's something bad.

This time, I'm not afraid I'll fall asleep on this cot.

I'm afraid I might never fall asleep again.

Corryn

Tez sits in the great hall with a plate of coagulated mac and cheese.

It's clumped up into a cold brick. He doesn't look

like he has taken a single bite. Instead, he presses a cold pack that can't be very cold anymore to his nose. He should use the mac and cheese instead.

I slide in with my own plate of slop and sit across from him. His eyes look dark and his skin has taken on the green tone of the lake. To say he does not look well is an understatement.

"I can't believe you barfed," I say. (Probably should have opened with "hi.")

"Hrm," he says. It's not really a word, just a noise.

"Actually, I *can* believe it," I say. "I've been there. One time when I was learning to 180, I wiped out so hard on my bike that I felt sick to my stomach. I didn't throw up, but I definitely thought I might."

"Hrm," Tez says.

This is pretty weird. From what I've observed, Tez is the type who likes to talk *a lot*, and all of a sudden, he's totally silent. The silence is kind of awkward, so I keep talking to fill the space. "I can't believe Knees kicked you. That's totally crazy. What was he thinking?"

All I get in response is another "Hrm."

Tez is not answering at all, just making this weird noise. It almost sounds like a snore.

"Don't fall asleep," I say, and laugh. "That's what

they always tell me when I fall off my bike. You know, if they're worried about concussions. They tell you not to sleep. Which is weird, you know, because for pretty much anything else wrong with you, you're supposed to sleep, to rest up and feel better. But somehow, no, if it's a concussion, it's like sleeping is pretty much the worst thing you can do."

"Thanks, I know," he says peevishly.

I preferred "Hrm."

"Jeez," I say. "Sorry. Just trying to make you feel a little better. That really was out of line that Knees kicked you like that! It's not fair. And Gavin, what a jerk. You know what makes me want to throw up? His cologne. I mean, it's like—"

"You think I care about Knees?" Tez says. He is not looking at me and is barely moving his lips. His jaw is clenched and his eyes are wild.

"You think I care about how Gavin smells? You think I care about getting kicked in the face? Faces get kicked, it happens. You know what *doesn't* happen? Rooms that change size and shape. Nurses who suddenly appear covered in blood!"

What the 7Up?!

"Did—did that happen?" I whisper.

Tez nods, gravely serious.

I swallow hard, then say, "Lakes don't try to drown you, either."

"What?" Tez puts his not-cold pack down hard. "Something happened during your swim test?"

"No," I say, lightly sarcastic. "My towel always tries to murder me when I'm at the beach."

Tez's expression changes. It's still dark, but now there's fear mixed in. "Corryn, there's something wrong with that lake."

I nod. "And with the clinic too, from the sound of it. And whatever it is, it's happening to both of us!"

"I don't know why you sound so happy about it," he says. "This just confirms that something is really messed up here."

"You got that right," I say. I poke the mac and cheese with my fork. It jiggles like it's doing a little dance.

Tez is right. I feel giddy all of a sudden. I should feel terrified, but instead I feel . . . well, yes, terrified, but also happy that I'm not alone. It's happening to Tez too. It's not just me.

And what's happening is not just plain old soul-killing parents-secretly-splitting-up summer camp. It's *special* summer camp.

It's *haunted* summer camp.

"This place is cursed," he says, not looking at me. He stares deep into the distance.

I waggle my eyebrows. "Look on the bright side. Curse is just another word for magic," I say.

"Curse," he says as he stares at me, "is just another word for evil."

8
Seventy-Two Hours

Tez

Insomnia makes a long night longer. Although technically, it's not insomnia, since I'm *trying* to stay awake.

I can't keep this up for the rest of camp, I know that. People have done experiments on dogs and rats, and they all discovered the same thing. At seventy-two hours without sleep, you start to freak out. At ninety hours without sleep . . . you die.

But I don't want to close my eyes and see the dripping nurse again, or those screaming faces in the fire.

Corryn's weirdly excited about all of this. Like it's an adventure or something. I sort of understand. With everything happening at home, she didn't want to come to camp in the first place, but I did. I've been looking forward to this all year.

It's just, I felt it in my defective heart: at camp, I didn't have to be the weird, sick kid. I'd get to be a regular kid. Old Tez Jones, literal happy camper!

Except Camp Sweetwater doesn't want me to be.

And that really, really makes me angry.

Because now, I'm afraid to roll over in my bunk and look at any of my cabinmates. Knees snores and Nostrils murmurs and sometimes Bowl Cut sits up, then lies back down. As far as I can tell, this is normal for them. But that doesn't make me feel better. Miss Kortepeter was perfectly normal too . . . until she wasn't.

"One lump," Knees mutters beneath me. "Or two?"

I hold my breath. Oh, God. What's happening? The bunk groans. It sounds like Knees is sitting up. His feet scuff the floor. Low, he mumbles, "Steep. Steep."

I can't figure out what he's talking about. Beating someone up? Throwing them off a cliff? I clutch the edge of my mattress. I don't want to listen, but I can't stop.

"Earl," he says. "The Earl!"

Then Bowl Cut flings his pillow across the cabin. "Shut up, tea party princess!"

In an instant, Knees comes completely awake. He

grabs the bottom of my bunk and hauls himself up. With a wind up, he flings Bowl Cut's pillow back at him. Then he picks up his flashlight and heads for the cabin door.

Gavin's still sitting awake out there and he bristles. "Where d'you think you're going, mate?"

"To take a leak," Knees responds with some sass. "You wanna watch?"

I don't hear Gavin's reply, because at the same time, Bowl Cut and I start laughing. Relief floods through me. Incredulous, I ask between snorts, "Was he really talking about *tea*?"

"Yeah," Bowl Cut says. (Even in the middle of the night, his shiny hair falls in a perfect loop around his head. Those are some legendary follicles, for sure.) "He says he watches his little sisters after school. They got some tea set for their birthday and that's all they wanna do."

One lump or two. Steep. I get it now. Ha!

I slump onto my back, staring at the ceiling. All the terrible things I was reading into his words, and it was innocent. Kind of silly and cute even, now that I think about it. "I wonder if he dresses up."

Bowl Cut snickers. "He probably has a pink lacy Easter bonnet with little bunnies on it."

"He would probably look nice in it," I note.

"Shut up, Chickenlips," Bowl Cut says. I think he wants to throw his pillow at me, but he'd have to get out of bed to do it.

The thin mattress crinkles when I settle onto my back. I put one hand on the wall and one beneath my pillow. The laughter is still bubbly and nice, and the cabin feels warm and solid. It says, *You're safe here, Tez.*

It helps me clear my mind.

Even though I don't mean to fall asleep, I drift toward dreams. And in that hazy, in-between place, my brains offer up a suggestion. Everything started with the black, gnarly wood that Corryn brought back for our bonfire. We burned it, and . . . what? Did we wake something up? Set something free?

I don't know yet. But I'm sure of one thing.

We are going to need to get more of it.

June 8, 1983

Corryn

A mysterious note is scribbled on the chalkboard under DAY'S ACTIVITIES. It says "G.L.I.T.W."

It's the only thing listed for this morning. No crafts,

no swimming. Just a little bit of good old-fashioned G.L.I.T.W. I have no idea what it means.

We are all in the Great Hall for morning announcements. It's going to be a hot day; the sun is already pressing through the clouds and making a line of sweat appear on my top lip. I take a sip of metallic-tasting water from my canteen and await the revelation of G.L.I.T.W.

Gavin has borrowed Scary Mary's megaphone. In his other hand, he has what looks like an air horn. With a sharp blast, he makes everybody from Oak Camp clap their hands over their ears. Yup, that's an air horn.

Pleased that he has our attention, Gavin jumps up on a table and yells, "Get lost in the woods!"

No one moves.

"Get lost in the woods," he yells again into the megaphone, louder this time. Then he positively screams, "GET LOST IN THE WOODS!"

Is that today's activity? G.L.I.T.W.? It checks out. I feel a lump in my throat. This is *not* going to be fun.

"How do we play?" one of the boys near the front asks.

"Well," Gavin says. "Step one—now follow me here, love, as this is kind of tricky—is to GET LOST IN

THE WOODS!" He puts down the megaphone, waits a few seconds, then adds, "That's bloody it! That's also step two and step three and step four through infinity. I honestly don't know why you're all still sitting here!

"Get out there and get good and lost and make sure you're back by lunch. Last one back gets work detail."

Tez raises his hand. "If the object of the game is to get lost, then coming back last should be winning."

Without hesitation, Gavin holds up the air horn and blasts it right at Tez. I kind of expect sound waves to make Tez's hair fly back, like in cartoons. No such luck. It's just loud and Tez blinks.

Gavin lays off the horn long enough to say, "If I want your opinion, I'll chuck something at your head! Now"—he blows the air horn again, yelling at the rest of us now—"if you hear this, it means you're one of the last ones back and you should leg it."

He gets some confused looks. "Leg it means to, like, hurry up!" He blows the air horn again. It's so loud that it hurts my ears and scrambles my insides.

Nobody else can tell if Gavin is being serious or not. If I had to guess, I would say yes. But Tez had a point. The rules of this game (or is it an activity?) are kind of stupid. If you don't want work detail, just walk a few feet into the woods and sit down.

Not me, though. I'm gonna get good and lost. I pick up my canteen and head down the trail past the band shell. Beyond that is the woods. I could think of worse ways to spend the day, to be honest. I like wandering around in the woods, exploring new trails on Elliot, or going on adventures with Dad. I'm really good at it.

"Lots of iron in my beak" is what my grandpa always says. It's something to do with how homing pigeons supposedly have iron cells that work like a magnet or something like that. Homing pigeons make me think of home, and thinking of home makes me feel a little sad. A little lonely.

Forget that: I have lost to be getting!

I step off onto the dusty path while most of the rest of the campers are still shuffling around. I get a few feet from the crowd when I hear a voice from behind me.

"Hey, wait up!" Tez says. "I'll come with you. I have a compass."

"Don't need one," I say, tapping my nose. "Iron in my beak."

"Like a homing pigeon!" he says.

I smile. I mean, not *at him*, just kind of in general.

We walk for a while. We eventually do get into an area that's pretty woodsy. There are no more trails, but I can still hear some sounds of camp and splashing at the lake behind us. We keep walking. Not talking, just walking.

A little while later, we feel that deep stillness of nature. No car horns, no laughing, no splashing. Just the buzz of bugs and the trill of occasional birds.

We walk a while longer. Tez is taking the game seriously, I guess, as we are just about to get seriously lost. Farther and deeper into the woods until the trees black out the sky. The limbs are dark and gnarled, twisting and reaching out like the fingers of witches.

Without the compass or nose-iron or whatever, it's impossible to say which way is back to camp. The wind picks up and whistles through the trees.

"Oooh, this is creepy out here," I say. "We could get eaten by a wolf who approaches us under three oak trees."

"There are no wolves in this part of Ohio!" Tez says. "I don't know why everyone's so worried about wolves."

"I'm just joking," I say. I punt a stick farther into the undergrowth. "It's from *Little Red Riding Hood.* I was in the school play. Ahem. 'Grandmother's house is one quarter hour from here. Surely you know the place. It is behind a hedge of hazel bushes and under three large oak trees.'"

"Oh," he says. "Were you Red?"

"Nope," I say. The wind howls again. "I was the wolf."

I curl my fingers into claws and smile in a way I hope looks lupine.

Tez's face turns a little green. I punch him in the shoulder. "Relax," I say. "Just joking with you."

The wind moans again. I feel my heart beat a little faster.

"I guess we should talk about, you know, things," he says.

"Oh yes," I say. Tang curdles in my stomach; he'd better not bring up my parents. "Things."

"You know, I was thinking about the vision in the fire, and—do you know the Oracle of Delphi?"

"Um, I've heard of it," I say—this definitely isn't going where I feared. I'm not getting interrogated about my home life. Unfortunately, I have no idea where it *is* going. "The oracle's from ancient Greece. I'm not sure what—"

"Yes, well, Pythia, she was the oracle there, the one

with the prophecies. She would hear things. See things." Tez starts to lecture like he's teaching class.

"Okay," I say.

"She would see things *that weren't there*."

"Uh-huh."

"So, some people think that she was actually kind of, well, high. There were cracks in the rock where she would make her prophecies. Gas came up. Petrochemicals or something. Vapors. She hallucinated."

"You think she was huffing on rock farts?" I ask incredulously.

He frowns. "You don't believe it?"

"I don't know. It's not like I was there. I don't think I've ever heard the word *petrochemicals* before. And I definitely didn't know that the oracle was a lady."

"Why do you—"

I interrupt him before he can have a little goober fit. "What I *do* know about is what happened to me in that lake. I wasn't hallucinating. I felt something, Tez. That's not like seeing a face in the fire or hearing a voice. Something grabbed me. I *felt* something."

"You can have a tactile hallucination. It's, like, a thing. If you lose a limb you can still feel pain there. People feel bugs crawling on them."

I shudder, just a little. "It didn't feel like bugs!"

Helpfully, he adds, "When it does, it's called formication."

"I just said, that's not what it felt like!"

"Okay, okay," Tez says. "But there are reasons for everything. Physical reasons. Or chemical reasons. Or brain reasons. You know, there has to be a . . . a reason."

"Only one way to find out," I say. I point to a stick embedded in the mossy ground. It's dark and twisted, bent into a harsh angle.

"The weird wood," he whispers. He bends to inspect it.

I crouch next to him. Hesitating, I stare at the knotted twist of a branch. Then I touch it with a tentative finger. That sick, uneasy feeling creeps toward my knuckle and I pull my hand away.

"Cold," I say.

"Yeah," he says. "Should we burn it?"

A far-off air horn sounds. I guess we're in the running for last. We lost at Get Lost in the Woods.

Or did we win?

It's really, really hard to tell.

9
No Deux

Tez

I have a feeling that the punishment for losing Get Lost in the Woods is just a chore that Gavin and Scary Mary were supposed to do.

After lunch, they separate us from the rest of our cabinmates. Instead of going to the lake, we're marched down an overgrown trail near the senior side of the camp.

The woods close over us, and after a mile or two, we reach our destination. A rotten sign at the side of the trail reads "Primrose." That strikes me as a little weird. I mean, this sign is in the middle of nowhere, it's not painted in sloppy red paint, and it's covered in old-fashioned writing. Just past it, the path opens into a scrubby clearing.

It takes me a moment to realize this is an old part of camp that no one's using anymore. It looks like ours, with cabins on either side of the path. But they're not *quite* like our cabins. These have steep roofs and slate tiles, thick logs as pillars, and decorations around the opaque windows. They're ornate . . . and way older than the rest of camp.

The cabins' shutters are broken, hanging off the frames. The tiles on one roof are shattered, and the wood beneath has slumped like melted butter. The cabins' missing doors lean against the side of a supply building. The paint on them is thick, chipped, and bubbled.

Even from here, we can see dirt and leaves inside the cabins; plants grow and wind toward the ceilings. Everything is slick green—mold growing all over it. It's like the forest is trying to devour this place, bit by bit.

"What happened here?" Corryn murmurs.

Shaking my head, I reply, "Time?"

It's not just time, though. There's another big difference here. In the middle of the cabin clearing, there's a stone fire pit. And, at the far end, there are three wooden platforms. One of them is sloppily painted—dark brown? Almost black? I have no idea what they're for.

As we get closer, I wrinkle my nose. Our cabins have an old, sharp smell to them, but it fades when the windows are open. These cabins reek of age. It's thick in the air: decomposition and abandonment.

"All right, you tossers," Gavin says, jangling a ring of keys. "The job's this. You muck out whatever's in this supply cupboard. If it's dry, put it in a pile here. If it's wet, Mary and me, we'll burn it."

My mouth goes dry. This sounds like a trap. Or the beginning of a Stephen King novel. Cutting a look at Corryn, I ask, "Shouldn't we have masks or something?"

Most people don't think I'm funny. Scary Mary thinks I'm hilarious. Her shrill laughter rings out, and it doesn't make this abandoned camp less creepy. She falls all over Gavin, clapping him on the chest.

"Masks!" she gasps, her crunchy, hair-sprayed hair flattening against his shoulder. "Ickle Chickenlips wants a mask!"

"Yeah, he's a git," Gavin says. With one arm around Scary Mary, he yanks at the supply building door. The door squeaks a little but stays firmly shut. Trying again,

Gavin has to give up his armful of terrifying British counselor. Still, nothing.

Gavin's face turns red. I can't tell if it's embarrassment or exertion. And it's not that I want to help him, but I do sort of want to get this prize-slash-punishment over with, so Corryn and I can get back to the business of torching our demon wood.

Helpfully, I say, "The door probably swelled. Because of the moisture in the air. If we had a crowbar . . ."

"I'll show you a crowbar," Gavin threatens. He puts his foot on the doorframe and yanks again. Nothing. The third time, the door finally flies open.

Arms and legs pinwheeling, Gavin staggers back, then falls on his—I'll use his terminology—*arse*. Drops right down on it, and then tumbles back in the grass dramatically. Dust and gnats puff up all around him.

Corryn buries her laughter in her shoulder. Her whole body shakes. I'm not laughing out loud, mostly because Gavin knows where I sleep.

Scary Mary flings herself at Gavin but glowers back at us. "Quit gawping and get in there!"

Just loud enough for me to hear, Corryn asks, "Can I gawp and get in there at the same time?"

Snickering under my breath, I tell her, "I bet you can."

"Gawp, gawp," she replies, and disappears into the supply building.

I follow immediately. Even though there's a blast of old and moldy inside, it's not as nasty as I feared. Shelves line the walls, and boxes line the shelves. In the front, they're thick cardboard. In the back, wood. Fading marker on the cardboard boxes reads "43–44," "13–14."

At the same time, Corryn and I say, "Dates."

She looks at me, her freckled face crinkled in disbelief. "We're doing *paperwork*? At *camp*?"

"Technically," I say, tugging at the first box, "we're burning paperwork. Ooh, think there's something they're trying to hide in here?"

"Only one way to find out," Corryn says. She tromps through moldering piles on the floor to check out some of the older boxes. A tiny *ting* rings out when she flicks the brass-framed tag on one of them.

"1883," she says, impressed. Then she peeks inside and makes a disgusted sound. A foul scent rises from the box, threatening to engulf us, until she slams the lid closed. "I found what they're hiding. The deep, dark secret that rats like to eat paper. This one's all chewed up and full of mouse pellets."

"Should probably put that on the burn pile, then," I suggest.

"No." Corryn gasps sarcastically and crosses her eyes at me. "Really?"

It doesn't feel like she's making fun of me. It's like she's making fun *with* me. I cross my eyes back. "Um, duh, really."

Pretty soon, we're sorting boxes like nobody's business. Most of them are ruined, and they go in the burn pile. Every so often, Gavin stalks over to grab those, tossing them into the blaze he and Scary Mary started in the stone pit.

A few of the boxes go into the keeper pile, mostly full of old receipts. On the top of one typewritten sheet from 1923, it says "For Market."

"Corryn," I say in my very best worst British accent. "Be a lamb, dear, and run to market for me!"

Looking up from her box, Corryn boggles at me. Then her slow smile starts to grow when I read on.

My voice rises, and I start to sound like an old lady with a speech impediment. "First, you'll need to see the cheesemonger, of course! Two five-pound wheels of their best CHEDDAH!"

"Oh, the children loooooove cheddah cheese," Corryn says. Her accent is as good as mine. So, terrible. But hilarious.

Flapping the list, and ignoring the edges that crumble away, I read, "And of course, we'll be wanting some ten pounds of the butcher's freshest tripe!"

"What the heck is tripe?"

I break my accent to whisper to her. "Guts. Intestines."

"They ate guts?! At camp?! Grody!" Flinging herself back in disgust, Corryn knocks one of the boxes onto the floor. It cracks, and its contents spill out at her feet.

Suddenly, the shed goes dark. Scary Mary fills the doorway, her face twisted like a third-grade pottery project. Her voice goes hoarse and growly when she screams, "Shut your gobs and get back to work, both of you!"

"I'll get back to work," I mutter after Scary Mary vacates. "But my gob remains open! Everything that's currently open on my body is going to stay that way."

"Gross," Corryn laughs.

I'm trying to figure out how that's gross when Corryn hands me something from her box. "Check this out!"

It's a slender book, richly bound. The front says CAMP SWEETWATER 1883, the letters pressed deep into the leather cover and embossed with gold. This looks just like a school yearbook, except thinner and way fancier.

Huddling close together, Corryn and I flip through the pages. The paper smells bittersweet—not archival quality—but the images are barely faded.

"Look at that hairdo," I say, pointing at a girl with hair swept into a giant bun thing. She has little curls at her ears, and bangs that look like she cut them herself, not that I ever did anything like that. (And then had school pictures taken. A picture that may or may not hang above the stairs in my house.)

Corryn snorts. "What the heck is she *wearing*?"

"Looks like a bathing suit," I say, examining the picture. "Those are bloomers, and I think she's holding a bathing cap."

Corryn gives me a look, like she's glad for the answer, but sort of sad that I'm strange enough to know it. Then she shakes her head at me, turning back to the yearbook. Studying the photo, she snorts and repeats, "Bloomers."

I laugh softly. We're either becoming allies, or going

crazy together, which is called *folie à deux*. You can pronounce *deux* like "duh," so it really fits.

Corryn turns the page and goes pale. Twisting toward me, she exclaims, "No freaking way!"

Her thumb partially covers the picture; when she shoves the yearbook at my face, I get a better look. "What is it?"

"The Old Lifeguard, Tez," she says impatiently. "The one that dragged me out of the lake. That's *him*!"

I shake my head in disbelief. "That's not possible. This yearbook is from *1883*. A hundred *years* ago."

"Dude, I can count," Corryn says, jostling against me again. "But I'm telling you, that's him. He was at the lake today. Him *and* his creepy mustache!"

Where's science right now, when I need it? I didn't see the guy, so I can't argue facts. I mean, besides the fact that there's probably a retirement age for lifeguards, and it's significantly less than a hundred years old.

All of a sudden, flipping through this yearbook is quiet and serious, no matter how funny the clothes and hair are. The whole place was girls-only back then. Our campcestors pose in stiff costumes for swimming, riding, archery. Face after face in fading brown ink gazes at us from the past.

"Look familiar?" Corryn asks, stopping on a snap of a cabin grouping. "That's here."

Back then, the cabins looked like gingerbread houses, sparkling and perfect. I can't even imagine them in color. They're just pale beige on dark brown, a fairy-tale village in the deep, dark forest.

When Corryn and I turn a page, we gasp at the same time.

Three campers stare at us from the back page. They smile, their eyes bright. They hold hands and wear flower crowns; they look happy. So different from the last time I saw them.

"The faces in the fire," I say numbly.

Corryn is a weird shade of greenish-gray. "They do kind of . . . resemble them."

The knot in my throat keeps me from talking at first. My voice comes out creaky. "Something bad happened here, a long time ago. To them."

"How do we find out for sure, though?"

Knitting my brow, I look out the door toward the fire. It seems a million miles away. Cold sweat crawls down my back.

Gavin and Scary Mary stand off in the tree line, trading something back and forth. They're paying absolutely no attention to either of us. We could be in here selling secrets to the Soviets and they'd never know.

That piece of black, gnarled wood is tucked into my rucksack. I collected it on purpose, and now I have thrice the reasons to burn it.

First, to see if the visions happen again. But now, second, to compare the faces in the yearbook to the faces in the fire.

There's a mystery afoot, and wood plus fire equals clues. Terrifying clues, but nevertheless. We have to do it.

Corryn

"Are you thinking what I'm thinking?" Tez asks.

I doubt it, because to be honest I don't even know what I'm thinking. This has crossed over from the curious to the confusing to the bizarre. I guess Tez is right. There are reasons for everything. There have to be. Chemicals or insanity or . . . something else.

What's happening to us *seems* crazy. But I don't feel crazy. I feel as normal as ever. And here are those three faces in the yearbook staring back at me. Three kids. Three very real kids. At least, they *used* to be.

"Gawp, gawp," I say.

"What?"

"I don't know. Just tell me what you're thinking."

Tez leans in close and puts his hand over his mouth.

"What are you doing?" I ask.

"I'm preventing detection by blocking the possibility of lipreading," he whispers.

Which is funny, because no one is watching at all.

"We burn the weird wood," he says. "Right here, right now." He points to the fire, which is still blazing enthusiastically in the clearing. It lets out a loud *pop!* and I almost jump out of my skin. "We have these pictures, right? We see if the faces come back. If they do . . . well, at least we'll know the vision has something to do with the burning wood. Maybe it's like the oracle, with the gases and such. Maybe it's something else. But we'll get there when we get there. At least we can establish cause and effect."

"What happened to 'there's a reason for everything'?" I ask.

He shrugs. "Same idea." He takes the branch from his rucksack. It might be my imagination, but it's crackling with energy now. It gives off a low hum, like when you hold a shell to your ear so you can hear the ocean.

Only what I'm hearing now is not the ocean. It's voices. I swear to dog, it's voices.

bloodwe'llbebloodsistersforeverbloodforeverblood-sistersforever

Tez resumes his lecture, blabbing over the whispers. "I mean, I know it's not from a typical deciduous tree, but—"

Seized by I-don't-know-what, I grab the wood from his hand and chuck it into the flames.

"Whoa," he says.

"Whoa," I agree.

He opens the yearbook to the page with the pictures of the girls we recognized from the fire. We prepare to wait, to compare the vision in the fire with the very real faces on the page.

But nothing happens.

No faces appear. The fire just burns along happily, burbling and turning the old musty files to ash.

Then everything goes black. Wait. No. That's not quite right. Everything also goes bright. Everything goes somehow black and white, blinding white and total darkness in one baffling moment.

My ears fill with a muffled squeak and my head feels like it's going to burst. I try to turn, to see if Tez is having the same experience, but find that I can't move my head. I can't move my head, I can't move my arms, I can't move my legs.

I can't move at all. I'm totally paralyzed! What is happening?!

Shapes appear in front of my eyes, replacing the bright darkness with shadowy forms. Like a camera snapping into focus, the shadowy forms become vivid. Standing in front of me, on the wooden platform, are three tents.

When did those get here? They're old tents, ancient really. They're just green cloth pyramids, held up by a single post. But the strangeness of old tents fades in importance when the screaming starts.

foreverforeverforeverforeverforeverbloodsistersforever

The screams are filled with unbearable sadness, and rage and . . . and then, like a switch being flipped, they stop.

Three girls appear in the middle tent, their faces shiny with sweat. They wear nightgowns, torn and tattered. They move their mouths as if trying to tell me something, but all I hear are whispers.

bloodsistersforeverFOREVERBLOODSISTERS-FOREVERforeverforever

It's the girls from the yearbook.
It's the girls from the fire.
The girls who were girls in 1883.
Are somehow here *now.*
Which isn't possible.
It isn't.
Right?

10
The Year of the Evil

Tez

My whole life, I've always known that I could die.

I never really *understood* that, though. I've felt danger—from a heart beating too fast, burning up inside my chest. A heart that could stop.

But most kids don't die. They just don't. Except now, at Camp Sweetwater, I have to face the truth:

Sometimes, they do.

These girls did. I'm sure of it. There is no other explanation for what I just saw.

These girls were *ghosts*.

Corryn stands next to me, trembling and shiny with

sweat. I can move again. How long have we been frozen here like this? I can't even tell.

"Did you—" she tries to ask, struggling to form the words with her parched lips.

Nodding, I stare into a fire that's just a fire, into smoke that does nothing but swirl into the sky. "I saw it."

"Holy macaroni," Corryn says. It's a mixture of terror and awe.

I think it's time to get super scientific so I don't go crazy. That's it. Scientific method all the way. That, and mindlessly going back to the storage building to finish clearing it out.

Science says Corryn and I can now reliably replicate some of our earlier results (cursed black wood + fire = terrifying visions). Now we have to expand our research.

More data:

The third platform in Primrose Camp, with its dark, uneven staining—something terrible happened to three campers, right there, one hundred years ago.

"Let's finish this," Corryn says. "Then we can get on to more important things." She doesn't sound excited, and I don't feel it. But we edge away from the fire and face the supply cabin again, together. This time, I go into the back, and Corryn takes the front. She can chuck a half-empty box way farther than I can.

"1863 to 1883," I say as I finish carrying out the first set of wooden crates. I line them up in the keeper pile.

"AHOY!"

A box goes flying past my head. Do I duck? I do not. I clutch my chest and whip around to watch its trajectory. When it crashes directly into the fire, Corryn leaps up and shouts, "Three points!"

I can't help it. I laugh. I laugh in a place of evil, and Corryn grins at me. She has a cocky look on her face and a hand on her hip. She says, "How about that?"

And I say, "You have an amazing natural grasp of physics and geometry."

Then her *face* says, "Okay, nerd," and we get back to work.

Sweat soaks our T-shirts. Dirt, dust, and cobwebs stick to our damp skin. But we manage to get the rest of the boxes pulled out—burned or stacked. As Corryn puts down the last one in our keep pile, she squints at it. "Huh."

"What?"

Gesturing at our collection, she looks to me. "There's a gap. A regular one. Every twenty years."

I come to stand beside her, and she's totally right. There it is, written in different handwriting across the years. Active files for twenty years, then nothing for twenty years. Files for the next twenty and none for the two decades after that. "The gap is real . . ."

"Mm-hmm," she says, elbowing me gently.

"But why?" I ask. I mean, if the faces are from 1883, it makes sense they'd close the camp after that, but—"

"Wait," Corryn interrupts. "What if a lot of something terrible happened here? On, like, a schedule? Like, every twenty years?"

I rub my chin and my brain chugs into overdrive. It's plausible . . .

"You'd think my dad would mention *that* when he was selling me on this place. Thanks, Dad!"

I snap my fingers. Her dad. That was the answer! Obviously!

Not Corryn's father personally, although I'm kind of mad at him on her behalf. But an old guy. Or an old lady. Camp Sweetwater has tons of them. The cooks and the senior counselors and the directors! We need somebody geriatric enough to remember the *last* time the camp was open. Someone who can tell us about the horrible things that happened here, either before they came, or after they left. We should ask one of them.

I'm *going* to ask one of them.

After we finish clearing out the boxes, Gavin and Scary Mary tell (okay, more like bark at) us to get back to camp. I am about to ask Corryn to go with me to the Great Hall to question adults when Scary Mary materializes from out of the blue. I let out a tiny yelp. I can't help it. She's terrifying! She steps between us.

"Get on to washing up. You can snog your boyfriend later," Scary Mary says, and it turns out that she doesn't need her megaphone. She's naturally so loud that everybody within three hundred yards of us turns to stare.

Face scarlet, Corryn mutters something to me as she goes. Either it's "Tell Elliot I loved him" or "I'll see you at dinner." But either way, it's a goodbye that leaves me standing with Gavin and a blush of my own.

I don't know what snogging is, but it goes with boyfriend, and that makes me squirm. I'm a *boy*, and I'm Corryn's *friend*. It doesn't become a compound word at any point, and I'm pretty sure she would agree with that. And also, she obviously already has a boyfriend—Elliot. Whoever he is.

"Go do something with yourself," Gavin says, and walks away. The back of his camp shirt is sweaty in a big V, with extra Vs under each armpit. Hopefully, he's going to change into a dry shirt. But wherever he's heading, it's without me.

I think it's probable that Gavin didn't take this job because he likes kids. Call me crazy, but it's just a feeling I have.

A hand falls on my shoulder, and fortunately, it's attached to an arm. To Mrs. Winchelhauser's arm, actually, which is fine as arms go. It's got an elbow and a wrist and all five fingers.

"Do you know where you need to be?" she asks me kindly.

Honest, I tell Mrs. Winchelhauser, "I have no idea."

She gives me a little tug and we start walking toward the main part of camp. "Let's see, have you finished your swim test?"

"I haven't, actually," I say. "I got kicked in the face and chundered on the dock."

"Pardon me?"

Oh, yeah. I translate from Gavin to grown-up-ese. "I threw up."

"How unfortunate. But why don't we start at the

dock, then?" she asks, but it's not really a question. I don't feel like I could reply with, like, an overwhelming desire to go play board games or weave some lanyards and expect her to agree it's a better plan.

As we head for the beach, I ask her with tons of subtlety, "Soooo, did you work here in 1963?"

A gurgly sound catches in her throat. "Uh, no. But I was a camper here then."

"Awesome," I exclaim. I slow my pace, just enough to give me time to question her better. Rubbing my hands on the sides of my shorts, I think about my next question before I ask it. You can't go from "hi, how are you" to "tell me about the gruesome murders in Primrose Camp" in one sentence. Even I know that.

Mrs. Winchelhauser smiles, extra pleasant. "Why do you ask?"

Oh, good! A nice easy entrance. Thank you, Mrs. Winchelhauser, esteemed camp director and friend to all. "Well, I was wondering why they shut the camp down afterward."

Mrs. Winchelhauser seems to be doubling her pace to make up for my halving it. "There were a lot of reasons, I suppose."

Aha! That's the kind of answer grown-ups give you

when they don't want to tell you the truth. This causes her to drop in my esteem somewhat. She's selling me a load of bull right now, and it's not even wholesale.

That leaves me no choice. I have to push my luck, and adults really don't like it when I do that.

"Well, what are some of them? The reasons, I mean."

She doesn't answer immediately. Then when she does, her voice is clipped. "There weren't going to be enough campers coming back to pay the bills."

"And . . . ?"

Her hand tightens on my shoulder. Her nails aren't long, so the fact that they dig into my skin says something. "And that's it, really."

"That's just one reason."

When she laughs, it's an empty sort of sound. "I guess it is."

We reach the edge of the beach, and she starts scanning around. I think she must be looking for a lifeguard, or somebody in charge of water activities. I step in front of her, squinting up and trying to make her meet my eye. It's kind of stupid to try; pretty much every girl in the world is taller than me. Mrs. Winchelhauser is no exception.

"It seems like this camp opens and closes a lot."

"Why would you say that?!" Mrs. Winchelhauser yelps.

Now, at this point, I can lie. Or I can tell the truth. Sometimes I'm bad at what my mom calls "reading the room": knowing when people want me to say things or when they want me to shut up, or when I should be informal instead of formal.

But I know for a fact that telling the camp director the truth—that Corryn and I are being haunted by three bloody, screaming campers—will land me back in the nurse's office, at the very least. I go for subtle again. "We just noticed it when we were helping in Primrose. 1863 to 1883, then bam, closed. Open 1903 to 1923, bam, closed . . ."

"Things happen, camps are expensive," Mrs. Winchelhauser says, cutting me off. She waves at a woman in the distance, her arm pumping ferociously. It looks like she's trying to get away from me, so I go for it, big time.

"Like the thing that happened in Primrose Camp, way back when?" I ask.

Mrs. Winchelhauser looks like I slapped her. Which I did not.

I'd never hit a girl. Or somebody with glasses. Or

anybody at all, really. I'm a lover, not a fighter. (I'm not a lover either. But I'm definitely not a fighter.)

Her tawny skin goes gray, and she swivels her head around to look at me. Even though she's narrowed her eyes, I see worry in them. And something else—something darker. Her voice is low and certain. "I don't know what you've heard, but whatever it is, you should forget it."

"I haven't heard anything—"

"Good," she says, cutting me off curtly. The woman she waved at approaches, and I recognize her as the female lifeguard from my first, failed swim test. Before she arrives, Mrs. Winchelhauser squeezes my shoulder again. "And whatever you *didn't* hear?"

I swallow hard. "Yes?"

Her eyes darken even more.

"Keep it to yourself," she warns.

Corryn

I can't believe it's only been two days since I waved goodbye to my parents.

Camp's been . . . interesting. And exhausting.

I finally have some time to myself, alone in the

cabin. Ew and Hairspray and Braids are all up in the showers. Mary is probably snogging Gavin somewhere. (Snogging means kissing in British-speak. This, I now know. Can't say I didn't learn anything this summer!)

Flopping back on the bed, I make myself comfortable. I'm kind of sweaty, but I don't want to shower. I plan to get up early to do it. I don't mind getting up early, and then I don't have to shower with an audience.

Plus this time alone is really nice. Time to think.

The sun starts to set, and the heat of the day steps aside for the cooling kiss of night. The smoky scent of campfire kindly curls in through the window. I feel relaxed for maybe the first time since I've been here. I grab a pen and paper and lie back on my pillow.

I don't know what to write. Tons to say, but the words just aren't here. *Hey, Mom and Dad. How is the divorce going? Didn't realize I knew about that, huh? Do I get to pick where I live, or are you going to flip a coin? Camp is okay, not that you care. Food isn't bad. Counselors are British and mean. People keep telling us to "get physical," like they're mega original. Oh, and there is probably an unspeakable evil haunting this place and trying to kill us. Okay love you! Kiss your lawyers for me. xoxo Corryn."*

I'm tired, worn down by hauling papers from the

camp and drowning in evil visions of the past. Not to mention a full slate of tennis and swimming! My mind races, turning over on itself. Full day. Busy day. I'm really bad at tennis, by the way. My eyelids start to feel heavy and my thoughts swirl like they do sometimes right before sleep.

Tennis.

The tennis instructor, a tall redheaded guy named Örn Odinson, either really likes me or hates me. He seemed determined to make me into a star tennis player, my glaring lack of talent to the contrary . . . Ha ha, that sounds like something Tez would say. His voice is getting into my head.

One of those camp things, I guess. Like how Ew and Hairspray have started doing the exact same laugh. They sound like hyper chipmunks. And they do it all the time, whether there is evidence of humor or not.

I feel myself dozing off, and then snap wide awake.

At first, I swipe my hands down my arms. My brain worries about bugs first, then notices another danger. There's a presence in my cabin. Someone here who doesn't belong.

I can feel it. I'm being watched.

How can the mere presence of eyeballs pointed in

your direction be felt? Maybe not everything in life has a simple explanation. Maybe there are some things that science can't touch. And I'm not talking about evil spirits. I'm talking about evil men.

I sort of open one eye. I'm good at peeking out from behind my eyelids so it looks like my eyes are still closed.

There, poking his mustache into the window of my cabin, is none other than Old Lifeguard! I track his dark eyes as they peer around the room. He's checking every bunk with disturbing intensity. He has no idea that I'm here!

A few seconds later, he moves on. What was up with that?

I scoop up my stationery and decide to follow. I feel like a detective. Nancy Drew and the Case of the Pervy Lifeguard.

I keep a safe distance but stay close enough to observe. It's not too hard. Nancy would be proud.

There are lots of campers around, throwing frisbees, strumming out-of-tune guitars, braiding each other's hair, laughing. I'm jealous. They are happy, carefree. They have no idea. They haven't seen the things I have.

I follow the Old Lifeguard as he makes his nefarious rounds. He's poking his mustache into the window of each and every cabin. Real casual like, nothing to arouse suspicion.

But what the heck is he doing? He's supposed to be guarding lives in the water, not spying on them on land. I get a lump in my throat remembering the yearbook.

He was at this camp in 1883. This guy should be beef jerky, dead and buried, but there he is, creeping all over like a centipede. He was here a hundred freaking years ago, the same year as the screaming girls. The same year as the blood.

The same year as the *evil.*

He was here, way back then.

What is he doing? Looking. *Hunting?*

I shudder. Did he have something to do with those girls and whatever happened to them?

Worse—could he be searching for a new victim?

11
J'ai Faim

Tez

Three facts keep me awake.

One, something terrible happened at Camp Sweetwater in 1883. Two, I suspect more bad things happened in 1963, when Mrs. Winchelhauser went here. Whatever it was, people don't want to talk about it. Three, whatever it was—*it* does.

It's talking through screaming faces in fires, and bloody nurses who disappear. It's shrieking with practically biblical swarms of pests. It's begging Corryn and me to pay attention, by nearly drowning her during her swim test and paralyzing us both to show us the past in a haze of smoke.

The possibilities make me toss and turn. I skim my hand against the wall. There are words and dates etched into it. These are the memories of campers who slept in this very place, years or decades ago. (Based on the smell, probably on this very mattress.)

Even if we say that we triggered the visions with the fire by burning that wood, what happened in the infirmary and at the lake had nothing to do with burning—or anything we did.

There are levels of science that haven't yet been explored. The rational explanation for these events is centuries away from discovery. Still, there is something I know deep in my core. Whatever happened in 1883—whatever terrible thing it was—caused a wrinkle in the universe. One that won't quite smooth out. Not even a hundred years later.

Whatever it is, it's reaching out for us.

It needs someone to know.

According to most accounts of these kinds of events, it wants us to set something right.

All of this is happening, to Corryn and to me. Since it is, I feel like we have a responsibility to investigate it. The science to explain it may not yet exist, but that doesn't mean we shouldn't try. And maybe with enough research and consideration, we can appease it. We can make it stop.

I seriously want to make it stop. Nothing weird happened during my swim test, but I still don't want to go back in the lake. The water just feels like a threat. And on top of that, my stomach churns when I think about getting hurt or sick, and having to go back to the cot in the infirmary.

The darkness in Camp Sweetwater is oozing over everything. Pretty soon, we won't want to leave our cabins at all. That's a problem for several reasons, including one big one: girls aren't allowed in the boys' cabins, and Corryn is really kind of cool. I want to keep hanging out with her.

I like Bowl Cut and Knees and Nostrils just fine. But Corryn is smart, and knows weird stuff just like I do, and she makes me laugh. Sometimes, I even make her laugh, which never happens with people at home. That means, if I want to hang out with her, I have to find a way to smooth out the wrinkle.

Bowl Cut sits up abruptly in his bunk. He's done this before. It's like his version of sleepwalking or something. Rolling over, I dangle my arm over the side and watch him.

"You awake?" I ask.

His eyes are open, but he doesn't answer. For a long moment, he sits there, kind of glowing in the dark. He's super pale, and standing around in the sun hasn't tanned him. It's just turned him into a freckle farm.

His hair is so spectacular, it even gleams in the moonlight. It falls into place perfectly.

Swinging my arm lazily, I say, "Lay back down."

For a second, I think he's going to. He leans back, but then he stops at a crazy angle.

Seriously, it's an acute angle; it can't be more than sixteen degrees between his back and the bed.

Without killer abs, it's physically impossible, and let's be honest: Bowl Cut doesn't have killer anything but bangs.

"Bowl Cut?" I ask, dread slipping over me. "Hey—Graham!"

Rising like a vampire from a coffin, Bowl Cut stands supernaturally straight.

I gasp, but I can't get a full breath. My throat is choking off all air; all I can do is watch as something moves Bowl Cut like a chess piece through the cabin.

He doesn't walk. He glides, his feet motionless. And

he makes no sound. As he drifts across the bare floor, moonlight falls on his face. It's empty in the worst way. His eyes are open but unfocused. His mouth gapes. He looks . . . I don't want to say it . . . but he looks dead. He looks like the pale, gray corpse of Bowl Cut, risen from his grave.

The only noise in our cabin is the whistle of Nostrils' nose as he inhales, and the box fan whirring. There's also the pound of my heartbeat, but I'm the only one who can hear that. Uneasy, I grab the side of the bunk and drop to the floor. The thump echoes. It's deafening to me, but nobody wakes up.

Not even Bowl Cut. He slides in front of the cubbies we keep our bathroom stuff in. The lights above us tick and flicker. They don't turn on. They just crackle with electricity—I feel it on my skin.

Something bad is going to happen. I sense it; I know it.

I try to get to Bowl Cut, to pull him back. But as soon as I hit the edge of my bunk, the cabin stretches out, impossibly long. Bowl Cut is suddenly miles away from me—too far for me to reach. And I feel the grip of cold hands around my ankles.

Every time I try to scream, I make nothing more than

a faint squeak no louder than Nostrils's nose whistle.

A sharp, electric buzz fills the air. At first, I think the lights are going to explode. But then I drop my gaze and realize what's really happening.

Gavin's electric razor has drifted off the shelf. Its cord hangs like a black snake, and I hear the metal prongs of the plug scrape-scrape-scrape across the floor. The razor rises up, heading right for Bowl Cut.

"No," I wheek out. I sound like a frightened guinea pig as I struggle to get my voice. "Stop!"

It doesn't stop. It cuts a furrow all the way around Bowl Cut's head. The stubbled trail it leaves is even paler than his regular skin. Tufts of auburn hair float to the ground in slow motion.

The razor cuts on. It doesn't rotate; Bowl Cut's head does. It turns so sharply to face me that I'm afraid his neck might break.

What if it did break? What if Bowl Cut died because Camp Sweetwater has a secret? That question burns in me, it burns me up. It incinerates the knot in my throat.

Finally, I manage to scream, "Gavin, help!"

The clippers fall to the floor. They clatter at Bowl Cut's feet as he looks around in confusion. His bald patches have streaks of blood trickling down from nicks left by the blades. Nostrils and Knees startle awake.

Everybody starts talking at once, including Gavin, who jumps out of his bunk, pulling up his boxers. If he wasn't sleeping in them, I don't want to know.

"What the bloody—" Gavin starts, and then his accent gets so thick, I can't understand him. It's definitely cursing, but too exotic to make out. His voice breaks when he shouts, "What did you do?"

Bowl Cut clutches his head in horror. "I didn't do it! I didn't do it!"

"You were sleepwalking again," Nostrils says. "Holy crap, dude, you're bald!"

He's not bald. Not entirely. And he wasn't sleepwalking.

But I say nothing, because what can I say? They didn't believe me about the faces in the fire. There's no way they'd believe Bowl Cut was under the control of an invisible force in our cabin.

Right here, in our cabin.

Where we are supposed to sleep.

But we're not safe here.

We're not safe anywhere.

Corryn

I dream of Elliot.

We're taking rad jumps off high ramps. We're doing 360s through the air. We're leaving all the chumps behind, sucking on our dust. Yeah! Then something wakes me from my peaceful slumber and disrupts my killer dreams.

Something moves in the room. All I can think is, it better not be a bug. Or an old, freaky lifeguard. I slowly open one eye, just the one. I am not quite ready to open both. It's still dark. But I'm pretty sure of what I'm seeing.

There's Ew, standing in the middle of the cabin. Is it the darkness playing tricks on me or is her head not quite right on her neck? She looks like a daisy with a broken stem.

She mutters, then speaks louder and louder. Words tumble out of her mouth. Strange words. It sounds like the same phrase, over and over again. Whatever it is, I can't make it out. It's like the meaning is just out of my reach.

Moving slowly, I slide to the edge of the bed. Sort of whisper-yelling, I call out, "Ew!"

Her body begins to rotate. Holy macaroni, she's

just hanging there like a broken marionette, her arms dangling heavily. Her head pitched to one side. It's hard to tell for sure in the dark, but I think her eyes are open. *I think*. They look like dark hollows in her face.

"Tammi," I whisper-yell again. As slow as I can, I reach for her.

The invisible line that suspends her jerks upward. Her body flops on it. Her toes drag on the floor as she drifts closer to me.

When I reach for her again, the invisible line tugs harder. Ew almost crashes into the ceiling!

FINE! I get it, evil entity, I won't touch her. But that doesn't mean I'll stop trying to help her! "Come on, Tammi, get up!"

The voice that comes out of her isn't hers. I'm not even sure it's human.

"Ecoutez!"

Wait, what? That sounds like French.

I know a little French. *Un peu*. Okay *un* very *peu*. Madame Anderson was not my favorite teacher. *Un peu* boring. Looked *un peu* like a department store cosmetics counter exploded on her face. Smelled *un peu* like she'd been rolling around in a vat of Jean Nate perfume.

Plus, Allen Brennaman sat next to me in French.

Allen Brennaman, a.k.a. Al the Man, a.k.a. the cutest boy in school. *Un peu* distracting. But I remember *ecoutez*; I heard it a lot. It means "listen."

Whatever's got hold of Ew won't let me touch, but it can't stop me from taking notes. I snag the stationery stashed under my bed. There is almost no light in the cabin. The moon is high and far away, hiding behind swirls of steel-gray nighttime clouds.

I fumble blindly for a pen. If I hold the paper up an inch from my nose I still can't read what I'm writing but can at least confirm that letters are filling the page.

"*J'ai faim, j'ai faim, où est mon sang?*"

Something like that. I am pretty sure that *faim* is hungry. *Faim* like famished. Hungry for what, though? What kind of ghost possesses someone just to ask for a snack? If you're hungry, get something to eat, dude. What? Are you going to go through the trouble of taking over a mortal's soul just to score some Doritos? Seriously, get it together!

What is *sang*? Think, Corryn! Think! But all my mind can conjure is the word *sans*, which means without. Hungry for without? Doesn't make any sense.

The only other thing my mind can conjure is Al the Man. Gah! Stupid Allen Brennaman! Stupid Madame

Anderson! Stupid French language and stupid Dorito ghosts.

"Gah! Stupid everything!" I yell.

Ew drops to the floor with a whimper. The sound is sickening. Her head cracks against the floor; her arms and legs splay out. All thoughts of stupid Allen Brennaman fly out of my head, because Ew looks dead. She looks *dead.*

Then suddenly, she looks up. Her eyes are eyes again. She's just a girl in pajamas, staring in confusion at the cabinmates she just woke up.

Someone flips a light on. Ew squints against the sudden and surprising brightness. The glow of the bulb is like a bucket of cold water. My heart still pounds, and the fear lingers. It's not like it was dark when I almost drowned in the lake. Light doesn't mean whatever was possessing Ew is gone.

"Did I fall out of my bunk?" Ew asks.

"Shut it!" Mary says. I look over. She has pulled a pillow over her head.

"But Tammi was, um, she was—" My voice is wobbling in my throat, teetering on the edge of crying. Angry tears. It's anger, I swear.

"That's a bead deduction," Mary says from under the pillow. "No nerd names in the cabin."

"Yeah, but something serious is—" I start to say.

"I *seriously* need my beauty sleep, you twits! I've got big Pancake Hut plans in town in the morning, and you lot will not make me miss my shuttle—or else!"

Ew hops up and shuts off the light and that's that. Her feet echo on the bunk as she climbs back into bed. When she gets there, she lays silently. She doesn't move, not even a little. She has no idea what just happened to her and . . . I'm not going to be the one to tell her.

Clutching my notes, I tuck them under my pillow. Tez has to see them; I have to tell him I heard the voice coming out of Ew's mouth—and it sounded familiar.

It whispered from the fire.

It whispered for *us*.

12
Ghostitos

June 8, 1983

Tez

I'm relieved that I'm not the only one who had a totally screwed-up night in Oak Camp. But I'm embarrassed that Corryn has notes, and all I can do is point to Bowl Cut's head.

Once Bowl Cut saw the damage, the jagged furrows cut through his hair, he let Gavin shave the rest. He looks like a broken man as he presides over his breakfast of four sausages and a mound of damp scrambled eggs.

"That's not the face of someone who's proud to fart into a box fan," I tell Corryn.

She hesitates, catching herself before she says "ew," and instead offers up a disaffected "Gross, Tez."

Obviously. But also hysterical, and part of Bowl Cut's personal comedy repertoire. Maybe it's just a boys' cabin thing. Snapping a slice of bacon in half, I pop it into my mouth and try to make out Corryn's handwriting. It looks like Sanskrit jotted down by an overcaffeinated Chihuahua.

"I kind of know what it means," Corryn says, pointing out a particularly scratchy line. "But I was sitting next to Allen Brennaman in class, and he was always saying these hilarious things under his breath when Madame was talking, so I don't remember . . ."

The bacon lands in my stomach the wrong way; acid churns. Allen Brennaman? I thought her boyfriend was Elliot. And what kind of name is Allen for a kid anyway? It's an accountant name. It's somebody who shows up to the Number Crunching Awards in a suit.

Allen. Ugh.

Corryn continues. "But I know for a fact that *j'ai faim* means I'm hungry, and *où est mon sang*, that's where is my something. *Où est mon stylo* means where is my pen, therefore . . ."

I give my bacon the side-eye and decide to cut a

piece of waffle instead. Maybe that will settle my green, burbly stomach. "It's easy if you know Latin."

With a cool, appraising look, Corryn puts the papers down and turns her attention to me. "*You* know Latin?"

It feels like a dare. I want to say yes, I know Latin and archaic Greek and Aramaic, and suck on *that* tail-pipe, Nonhilarious Allen in French Class. But it would be a lie, and while I'm not above lying, I am above embarrassing myself by trying to pretend I speak dead languages.

Clearing my throat, I say, "No, but I know a lot of root words. *Stylo* is related to stylus, which comes from the Latin *stilus*, and they all mean a kind of pen."

"Super great," Corryn says. "We don't need a pen. We need *sang*."

"Sanguine," I reply. "Really red. Exsanguinate, *ex*—to take out, *ate*—to do the thing . . ."

"Tez, if you don't do the thing . . ."

I lift my chin. "*Sang*. Blood. Exsanguinate means to take all the blood out of something, and Ew told you that she's hungry and wants to know where's the—"

"Blood," we both say together.

Dropping her fork, Corryn says, "That's messed

up! And here I thought she might just want some Ghostitos . . ."

"What is that even?" I ask her.

"Tortilla chips for ghosts, Tez! I mean, keep up!"

Now we both stare at breakfast, and now I want Doritos a little. I don't know why. My stomach is still uneasy, and I've already barfed once at camp. I don't want to turn into the guy that's known for puking. Chickenlips as a nickname is bad enough. Pukeface would be a definite downgrade.

"What are we going to do?" Corryn asks finally. She chases a sausage link around her plate with her fork. "Obviously, it's getting worse."

With a bravery I don't feel, I say, "We're going to figure out what's going on, and we're going to stop it. We are going to be the dry cleaners who take care of this wrinkle once and for all!"

"Dry cleaners?" she asks.

I nod. "To iron out the wrinkle—in the cosmos."

She blinks, waiting for it to make sense.

"It's an extended metaphor," I mutter. "But anyway, the plan is to find out what these ghosts or whatever are trying to tell us. Then, maybe, they can rest."

This awesome plan is absolutely foolproof, except nobody at camp is talking about what happened. We can't stop something we can't see. We can't anticipate something we don't understand. And that thing, apparently, hungers for blood.

"If this doesn't work, we may have to pretend we have mono until the camp director calls our parents and sends us home," I tell her. But I'm pretty sure Corryn's not interested in going home right now.

Finally spearing the sausage link, Corryn says, "If my dad were here, he would tell me to look it up. I think it's because he got suckered into buying a set of encyclopedias by a traveling salesman, but he's obsessed with having me look things up. Sometimes I'll ask how to spell a word and he'll be like, 'go look it up,' which is hard when you don't know to spell the word!"

"Well, typically you could begin by looking up the prefix and root word and . . ."

"Tez! Please stop."

"We could try to do some research, though," I say. "I doubt it's an accredited research facility, but I read in the *Camper's Guidebook* that there's a library here."

"The *Camper's Guidebook*. You read that thing?"

"There's some good stuff in there!" I feel myself blushing a little bit. Corryn laughs and throws a crumpled-up napkin at my face. I smile.

"Well, let's hope there's some good stuff in the library too," she says. She pushes back her chair and the metal legs grind like bones into the hardwood floor. With a crooked smile, she says, "I'll go get my card."

I resist the urge to tell her that, according to the *Camper's Guidebook*, library cards are not needed.

Corryn

Tez seems like the kind of guy who's at home in a library. I triple-dog-dare him to get cozy here, though.

The camp library is a stuffy, boxy lodge with the windows still boarded up. Thin fingers of light try to push through the cracks. They crisscross the space, golden motes suspended in them. They glow—barely. This building looks a lot like the rest of camp: rustic cabin, with a high ceiling and angular arches every few feet.

It has some of the basic library requirements: shelves, check. Cubicles that Tez informs me are named Carol (I told you, he's a weird dude), check. Magazines, check, in open boxes by the door, waiting to be shelved, and of course, books. Lots and lots of really, *really* old books, checkadelic. If it weren't for Cyndi Lauper on the cover of one of the boxed magazines, I'd think we had stepped back in time.

Here are the library requirements that are not met: no chairs, no lights, no way to breathe without one of those freaky, bird-beaked plague masks. (The only reason I know about those is because my dad used to be in the Society for Creative Anachronism, which is a fancy way of saying dudes who get together and play olde-timey dress-up. He loved it, but he said it came down to a choice: he could either have kids or a replica sword from the Crusades made of Damascus steel. Lucky me, I made the cut. Thinking about it now—with the divorce revelation? It's not actually that funny.)

Seriously, though, what is the deal with this place? The library's not open. Our bunk had serious issues. Half the other stuff in the camp brochure isn't open yet, either.

I was looking forward to Radio Free Corryn on 92 point 4, WSWT, but nope. Station isn't open yet. Neither is the newspaper or the technology lab. For real.

I step inside like I'm going to help, but I'm not. Come

on, anybody with two brain cells to rub together can take one look at this place and know it's a loss. Sure, I'd *love* to find *The Great Big Manual of Paranormal Activity at Camp Sweetwater*, but it's not gonna happen. At least, not in here.

I streak Superman's S into the dust on the card catalog, then turn to look at Tez. He pulled his shirt up to cover his face. Crouched like a crab, he creeps down the shelves to read titles.

The thin light shifts, and I catch something out of the corner of my eye. Something *moved*. Low, against the bottom shelf where Tez stirs the dust and ancient books about girls and their horses.

"Is that a bug?" I say, then immediately regret it. Tez laughs and says "Probably," and I start to itch. Stupid bugs.

All along the ceiling, fluffy, lacy cobwebs gather. Who knows what's alive in this place? My head spins. Oh man, I'm going cuckoo for Cocoa Puffs. Too much dust and not enough air will do that to a future BMX star.

Happy on his own, Tez pulls a book out. A puff of dust follows it, and he starts to cough. Every time he does, it stirs up more dust. Between wheezes, he holds up the book triumphantly. "*History of Sweetwater County.* I bet this has everything!"

"Rad," I say. "Can we get out of here now?"

In reply, the door slams shut behind me.

Spinning around, I stare. It took me and Tez both to yank that thing open. The frame was warped, just like it was in the storage building in Primrose Camp. So whatever just made the door close—it had to do it on purpose. Almost like it was waiting there . . . watching us. Waiting for the moment we wanted to leave.

"Uh," Tez says brilliantly.

"Yeah, no," I say, nice and loud. Marching toward the door, I grab the rusted handle. "I've had enough of your shenanigans, ghosts-or-whatever-you-are. You can just stop right now, because we're getting out of here!"

That's right, I tell 'em who's boss!

Except then I pull, and nothing. I jerk on the door with all my strength. It's like tug-of-war with a bull. Bracing my feet hard, I put my head down. Then I strain and yank the door with my shoulder. The door doesn't budge, but a sharp pain runs down my arm.

"Corryn," Tez says weakly.

"I'm doing this," I reply, and crash into the door again.

"Corryn."

"I said I'm—"

Tez cuts me off. "Corryn, turn around!"

Slumping against the door, I do.

Books drift off the shelves and through the air. Rolling onto their spines, the pages splay open. A breeze ruffles the pages—it's like people we can't see or hear are browsing all at once.

Then the books rise toward the ceiling. Their covers flap. Dust rains down like fine ash. It coats my tongue; I taste it when I breathe.

Tez's hair is really, really dark brown most of the time. Right now, it's gray, and his eyes are giant, dark circles in a powdered face. He looks like George Washington's ghost.

Still clutching the door handle, I slide to the floor. "Get low," I say, like I have experience with possessed books.

Just as Tez dips down, a thick volume fires off the shelf.

Fzzzzzz!

It whizzes through the air like a bullet. When it

slams into the opposite wall, it falls to the floor. The pages flutter, like it's wounded. Like it's *alive.*

Inching toward me, Tez murmurs, "What if I run at the—"

BAM! Another book plows into the cubicle right next to Tez's head.

My guts clench. I don't have time to take a breath, or to warn Tez to get even lower, when the next book shoots free. It *whams* into the door above me. I feel the sound as much as I hear it.

The book corpse drops on my head. The corner whacks me a good one, right behind my ear. Old, molded pages disintegrate all around me. Decay invades my nose.

Tez grabs one of the bookcases and sliiiiiiiides himself across the floor. Like, if he goes slow, nothing will notice him.

He's wrong.

A whole rack of yellowed paperbacks rise up. They fire at him all at once, like a shotgun blast. They whistle until they reach their target. Dime novel after dime novel explodes against Tez's exposed back. I lift my head as a hefty volume rises from the back table.

"Dictionary!" I yell, and hit the ground.

I cover my head like it's a bomb incoming. So does Tez. Just in time. The dictionary explodes somewhere above us. A rain of dust chokes us; book shrapnel pings off our arms and backs. Shredded pages flutter down, a soft, ominous snowfall.

The sound of fluttering books rises, buzzing now like hornets. Angry hornets—a whole nest of them. Another book zings across the room. *Bam!* Another—*BAM!*

In spite of this, Tez continues to slink. He yelps when a pinwheeling copy of *The Outsiders* slams into his head, but he keeps going. *Stay gold, Ponyboy!*

Soon, he's pressed right next to me, next to the door. The door that refuses to open.

"I have an idea," he says, trying to stuff the collection of junk he keeps in his pockets back down. He's got a compass, empty gum wrappers, a magnifying glass. I mean, why, even? Tez has never struck me as the kind of guy who burns up ants with a magnifying glass. "If we wrap my shirt through the handle and pull at the same time . . ."

I shake my head. "No way. It's stuck because it wants to be."

"It's a door," Tez says.

Whispering at him, I say, "*Haunted* door." Then my brain pukes up the best (read: only) option left in this situation. Shoving my hand toward him, I say, "Give me your magnifying glass."

Digging back into his pocket, Tez fishes it out. Suddenly, a picture book spins through the air like a throwing star. It goes right for Tez's wrist. The magnifying glass flips out of his hand. It skids across the floor, into the open.

Yeah, that's right, I think to the ghosts. (I'm smart enough not to mock them out loud.) *I know what you're afraid of.*

I roll onto my hands and knees. Then I crawl as fast as I can. As if sensing me, the card catalog's drawers open. Hundreds of three-by-five cards, neatly typed, spray into the air. Whooshing past me, they slice my arms and my legs, a zillion papercuts all at one time. My skin burns, but I grab the magnifying glass and hold it up.

One streak of light hits the glass, already thin, and now focused hard on the shredded paper that litters the floor.

That's when Tez realizes what I'm doing. He slides on his belly, gathering up huge handfuls of tinder.

Shoving soft, torn paper into the focused sunlight, he flattens himself and blows gently.

Whole sections of books fling themselves off the shelves. The cabinets and bookcases bang against the walls. It's like they're trying to tear themselves loose. One of the study tables rocks back and forth, then flips itself over. It smashes into the wall, exploding into sawdust and splinters.

"Come on, come on," Tez says urgently.

"Please work, please work," I mutter. It's not praying exactly. But it's not *not* praying. My arm shakes. Delicate threads of blood trickle down my skin. Now the card catalog itself starts to rock. If that thing hits us, we're done for.

It lunges, and screws in the feet scream. Another lunge; the screws fall out. They rattle across the floor as the catalog groans and wrenches itself free.

The catalog cabinet rises.

Then there's a hiss.

And a whuff.

"Fire!" Tez shouts joyously.

And with that cry, all the books above us drop. They smash down, banging off the tables and shelves and our stupid, dusty heads. The catalog stills; the shelves fall into place, motionless. The door clicks, and groans as it swings open.

"We did it," Tez warbles.

My voice is a little warbly too. "We did." I pause. "What have we done?"

"We set a library on fire!" Tez doesn't even sound conflicted. Probably because he's got a real good cut across his eyebrow. It actually looks pretty tough. Like Indiana Jones or something. He smothers the small fire, then crawls back over to me. "You're a genius. Whatever's behind this doesn't want to be destroyed, and you . . . you're a genius."

From a kid like Tez, that's a huge compliment. I thank him, and then shove him to the door. "No more investigating today, all right?"

"Agreed," he says. We stand when we get outside. But we can't help but look back. It looks like somebody threw a bookstore into a blender in there. Good thing they were already late opening.

Glancing down, I catch my breath. *History of Sweetwater County* lays at our feet. It's like a miracle we got it out of there. I bend to pick it up. But when my fingers brush the cover, it decays into dust. There's nothing left of it but the red and yellow stitching that used to bind the pages together.

Whatever we're dealing with is powerful.

It has rules.

I hate rules.

But this time, they might actually save us.

13
Ohio Twirl

June 9, 1983

Corryn

A normal day. No weirdness. No investigating. That's the plan for me and Tez.

We eat a normal breakfast, we do a normal craft (macramé plant holders), we have a normal identifying-poison-ivy session. Tez points out that lots of plants, Virginia creeper, for example, have three leaves, and that the childish rhyme is far from the only way to blah blah blah. But as soon as we step inside the Rec Barn for our afternoon activity, we're met with a weird, acidy smell. The horrible scratch of a record player greets us.

I can already tell: this is *not* going to be normal.

The music is way too loud—ancient and horrible. It's all screechy and scratchy violins, the same tedious rhythm on an endless loop. I could have brought my Rick Springfield 45s if I'd known there would be a record player. Anything would be better than this.

But while Rick Springfield is excellent for dancing, he's not excellent for *square* dancing! Which is, apparently, what we are expected to do.

What is this, the *eighteen* eighties? Ridiculous. I can't believe they are making us square dance. Who designed this torture?

A stench hangs in the air. This time, it's not even sweaty campers. It's from a fresh coat of paint being applied to the Rec Barn—inside and out. It seems like they're in a big rush to get it on because about eight camp staff members wield a brush or a roller.

What are they in such a big hurry to cover up? Even the creepy, peepy, pervy Old Lifeguard is there, now with extra creepy red paint dripping off his hands. He's not doing anything, though, just kind of staring at us. Awesome. I can't wait to clompy-stomp with him watching.

Winnie Shacklehoff, an art counselor with a dopey

black beret, is in charge. She's up in front, clapping along to the beat and stomping on the floorboards.

Some of the boys join in. They seem like they're trying to stomp right straight through the floor or maybe to shake the new coat of paint off the walls. If she doesn't settle them down, instead of a square dance, it's going to be a square riot. A square mob scene.

"Okay!" she shouts. Then she shouts it a few more times until the stomping ceases. She carefully lifts the needle off the record and the room goes quiet.

"Square dancing is great exercise, and more importantly, great fun!" She gives a huge thumbs-up to the crowd of campers who don't exactly seem to feel the same way. I look around and see Tez offering a weak thumbs-up in return. "Don't worry about who your partner will be, because we are going to be switching often. One of the great joys of square dancing is having lots of partners."

From behind me I hear a single syllable expressing what we are all thinking.

"Ew."

"Let's start with a basic step. This is called the Dixie Stomp! Let's go!"

Let's go indeed. Let's go as far as possible from here.

The Dixie Stomp is a one-person goofball dance, and from there we go to the California Twirl. This is one of those moves where the guy spins the girl by her hand. Why can't the girl ever spin the guy?! I'd like to do the Ohio Twirl, which I just made up. It's just me standing in the corner and slapping any guy who gets near me. Not so much twirl, but very Ohio.

Winnie pairs us indiscriminately. I end up with Nostrils, oh he of *my moms lets me watch every horror movie in the universe* fame.

"With a bow," Winnie yells, "Introduce yourselves to your partner!"

"Hi, my name is Nostrils," he says. "Nice to smell you." He inhales deeply. I guess some people are really embracing their camp names.

"I'm Corryn," I say, shaking his hand. "I don't have a nickname and I don't dance."

"Suit yourself," he says with a shrug and a smile. He starts to do-si-do. He's really got this down. Not only that, he appears to be . . . *enjoying himself.* His smile is kind of irresistible, and I find myself grinning back at him.

Braids, linked arm in arm with Bowl Cut (now

Chrome Dome) across the Rec Barn, catches my eye and mouths, "Kill me."

"California Twirl!" Winnie shouts, and Nostrils spins me around. I spin, but my stomach is a California two-steps behind me. I hope that lurgy feeling in my gut isn't going to turn into a Chesapeake Chunder.

Winnie yells "Change partners!" and Nostrils whips me across the room like we're wrestling. Dude is seriously intense when it comes to square dancing. Maybe next time, somebody should give him a list of do-si-*don'ts* before we start.

At the end of my twirl, I find myself linking arms with Tez.

Before I can say anything to him, he leans in close. "I'm racking my brain over here," he says. "We have got to get to a real library and find some real information. Newspapers! Microfiche!" He keeps dancing, not missing a beat.

Microwhat? I *am* missing a beat. Thinking about supernatural phenomena makes it hard to get my arms and legs situated properly for the twirl.

"Change partners!" Winnie calls again, and I find myself tripping over Tez's feet. He's got some serious boats. I crash into Bowl Cut, who stumbles and falls to the ground, splayed out like a pale, paunchy domino.

I try to California Twirl back to verticality, but gravity is winning its battle. Grabbing for anything to steady myself, I knock Tez off balance. Painfully slowly, Tez stumbles—and crashes into the wall. The freshly painted red wall.

The record player skips, and everyone in the barn turns their heads. Momentarily stuck to the tacky redness, Tez crumples in slow motion. Then he slides to the floor, leaving a streak where the paint had been.

The paint now, of course, is on Tez. It coats his arms and hands, and there's a bright-red splotch in the center of his chest. His face is also red, but I'm not sure if that's paint or embarrassment.

I step over Bowl Cut and hurry to help Tez up. I get there the same time Winnie does. She's all panicky—she probably didn't expect to have a lot of emergencies as an art counselor. Ha ha, welcome to Camp Sweetwater!

"Are you okay?" she asks, grabbing one of his slick, red hands to help him up.

"Should have stuck with lanyards," Tez says.

I laugh, the air shooting out of my nose in a loud snort. Winnie and I each grab an arm and carefully hoist him off the floor of the barn. Most of the campers have stopped gawking and have gone back to dancing. A couple of them are adding kung fu moves, creating a new kind of art form: square fu, the stompy art of face smashing.

I'm about to laugh for the second consecutive time—which would be a record at this forsaken place—when I feel it.

Eyes, staring at me.

From across the barn, the Old Lifeguard has me in his gaze.

I can't get out of there—I mean, get Tez to the infirmary—fast enough.

Tez

It's weird to shower alone in the middle of the day.

Not that I'm crazy about showering with people at night. If you think Bowl Cut lives in Gross-Out City in our cabin, just imagine what he does when we're all naked and no one's watching. None of his bunkmates will be spared our recurring nightmares from the experience.

But when it's full, the shower house doesn't echo. People sing and talk and laugh. It doesn't matter that the thin curtains that cover each stall look like they were last washed in 1963. Even though there are shadows and spiderwebs in the corners, it's not ominous. There's life in there.

Unlike now.

The dripping sound of a single faucet reminds me way too much of the day the infirmary tried to scare me to death. Mildew presses in, a dank kind of humidity that I can't escape. Above the sinks, polished metal mirrors distort my shape as I walk past them. I'm tall, I'm short, my head is cut off . . . ugh.

The curtains don't completely close on the first two stalls. There's a bunch of hairballs stuck to the wall in the third. That means I'm hitting number four, the darkest stall of all. Literally. The lights don't reach all the way back here.

Tossing my laundry bag on a hook, I strip out of my paint-soaked clothes. They drop at my feet, and they can just stay there. I don't know what kind of paint it is, so I'd better rinse them out before laundry day.

Flip-flops firmly on feet, I kick my clothes aside and grab my bar of soap. At a protective distance, I reach out with one tentative hand and turn on the tap.

Warm water sprays out in a majestic arc. Whoa. When everybody's washing at once, we get a trickle of almost lukewarm spit. This is an actual shower. A relaxing, good-for-thinking-about-stuff shower!

Maybe tripping in front of everybody in Oak Camp and face-planting in wet paint wasn't *that* terrible.

I step into the water and sigh. Yessss. Hot shower with water pressure. This is a treat. Hot shower with no guest appearances by Bowl Cut's butt, even treatier. It's the simple things in life, you know? Getting the last chocolate pudding at dinner, realizing that black thing on your leg isn't a tick . . . I relax into it, ahhh.

Then I glance down and recoil.

Blood!

I'm washing in blood. It pours out of the faucet, hot, human blood soaking my hair! Running down my face, down my arms. It races down my legs, down to swirl around my feet and into the drain. Agh!

But then I realize it's just the paint sluicing off my skin. With a merry gurgle, the drain swallows it all.

Stupid paint. Good riddance.

I turn to face the faucet, for two reasons. One, I need to rinse everything I just soaped up. And two, I want to make sure that the water stays water. Things in Camp Sweetwater have a funny way of turning out to be something else completely.

My mind wanders again. It's *really* weird that half the stuff in camp isn't open yet. My thoughts drift sideways to something else that's weird. Nobody said *anything* about the camp library being destroyed.

If you weren't there, if you hadn't seen the books tear themselves to pieces, you'd think it was vandalism. The worst kind of hard-core vandalism, because what kind of psycho deliberately hurts books?

And yet, there's been not one peep. From anyone. It didn't come up in the announcements at breakfast. Not even the newly broken window! The shards of glass are *right there* on the grass. But silence.

There are way more questions around here than answers. And are there really any answers that would make any of this make sense?

The shower curtain brushes against my calves, cold and damp. Reaching behind, I shove at it, although it's pointless, really. The hot water warms the air in the shower; that air gets light and rises.

That leaves room for denser, colder air to push in. And it does, taking the shower curtain with it. Science! It's basically the same thing that causes thunderstorms and tornadoes. High- and low-pressure fronts push into each other, creating a big, atmospheric merry-go-round (that sometimes ends with destruction).

Again, the curtain ripples against my legs. The cold, knobby hem draws against my calves like a finger; my heart pumps faster because my irrational lizard brain decides that a totally normal, absolutely ordinary phenomenon—isn't.

Firmly, I tell myself, this isn't like books sliding off the shelves by themselves. That's plainly impossible. Shower-curtain crawl, however, is *strictly* physics!

Annoyed, I shove the curtain back and in response, *it curls around my hand.*

There's a crawling, creeping feeling that burns through my heart between each beat: this happened to Corryn. In the lake. Her towel.

At the time, I barely believed her.

There's no time for guilt.

"Let go," I growl, and pull hard.

The curtain pulls back. Sharp and hard. It whips me around. It loops my body, tangling and binding me. It plasters against my face. Pinned to my thighs, my hands open and close helplessly. I can't pull this thing off.

Each time I turn, it gets tighter. Panicked, I even try dropping all my weight at once. It's a stupid, rotten shower curtain. It should tear off the rod like toilet paper. Or the rod should collapse!

It doesn't. I'm tangled and hanging in a shower curtain cocoon. It tightens like a boa constrictor. When I try to breathe, it's like sucking air through a straw. My head pounds. It feels like my brain is swelling. Pushing against my skull. Pushing my eyeballs out of their sockets.

My tongue pushes out, too big for my mouth. A thousand red-hot pinpricks sweep across my face as my feet lift off the floor.

Strange sounds surround me. Grunts, guttural and thick. A high-pitched whistle. I can't think. I can't think anymore, but I think I'm making those sounds. I think that's me.

The splash of water is far away now. Kind of pleasant. A white noise to go with the darkening in my head. Everything stops. Even me. I go still.

I'm dying.

14

Who Who Who vs. Cha Cha Cha

Tez

Ouch!

Something hard digs into my ribs. "Boy, what are you doing down there?"

Head throbbing, I raise my hand. Rubbing my face slowly, I open my eyes to a familiar face. Whoa, whoa, whoa! The Old Lifeguard stands over me, his whistle dangling from his neck like a pendulum.

His boot is in my ribs—definitely not a ghost. Yeouch!

I have to look around. It takes so long to blink my eyes. My throat is sore, and where am I? Slowly, I realize I'm lying on a cold concrete floor. I ache everywhere;

it's like I got hit by a truck. A very small truck, one that fits inside a camp shower. Running water splashes cold against my bare skin.

Wait . . . bare?

Jeez Louise, I'm naked!

Scrambling to cover my kibbles 'n' bits, I scrape my backside on the floor. Towel, towel, where's my towel? Oh, it's in the Old Lifeguard's bony, ancient hands. Awesome! With one hand still strategically in place, I hold the other one out. "Can I have that, please?"

He gives it to me, then turns his back.

At least I get to stand up with some dignity. My knees feel like rubber, and my head spins as I rise. Wrapping the towel around my waist, I find myself wishing I had another one. Or a robe. A big fluffy one. Maybe with a monogram on it.

"You wanna tell me what you were doing lollygagging and thrashing about in here?" The Old Lifeguard is a statue. He doesn't even glance back.

Quickly, I grab my laundry bag. Stuffing my soap and wet, paint-stained clothes into it, I say, "I just got dizzy."

"You sure about that?"

I duck my head and slip around him. When the

shower curtain brushes against me, a chill cruises down my spine. "Completely sure. One hundred percent."

The Old Lifeguard squints at me. "I know about your condition."

When he says it, it sounds ominous. It's not like a cheerful *Hey, I heard some interesting trivia about you!* It's more like, *I know something I can use against you.* I swallow hard, and my throat protests painfully. What does this guy want?

Backing away from him, I say, "Yeah, well, I'm fine. If I'd experienced any vasovagal syncope, I'd go to the nurse. But I didn't. That's why I'm going to go put on some dry clothes and get back to square dancing."

When the Old Lifeguard moves, I swear I can hear his bones groaning with the effort. He really is ancient. He looked like a grown-up in the yearbook, and that was a hundred (impossible!) years ago. Why would Camp Sweetwater hire this guy? (*How* could they hire him?!)

The Old Lifeguard keeps walking toward me. "They're not square dancing anymore."

My mouth goes dry. "Okay, then . . . I'll meet them at the nature center?"

"Kid," the Old Lifeguard says, walking past mirrors

that make him seem even more fun-house terrifying than he does on his own.

The thin, yellowish light thrown off by the bare bulb above us does him no favors, either. It darkens every single line in his face. It outlines his dingy teeth. One of the top ones is chipped. "They're getting ready to head to dinner."

My stomach growls and goes sick at once. When I came up here, it wasn't even lunchtime! I've been passed out in my birthday suit for five hours?! Nobody noticed I was missing?!

Clutching my laundry bag, I say, "Thennnn I guess I'm gonna go get dressed and head to dinner."

"You do that," the Old Lifeguard says. Then he adds, "And keep your nose where it belongs."

It feels like a slap. I wasn't nosing. I wasn't doing anything weird or inappropriate or even questionable. I was a man, alone in a shower, washing away my worries and some stinky red paint until the decor started strangling me! "I was just taking a shower!"

"And look what that got you."

The Old Lifeguard brushes past me and heads down the path toward the Great Hall. I boggle after him.

And then my brain clicks and thoughts start to flow together. Mrs. Winchelhauser kinda warned me to keep my mouth shut. Now this weirdo warns me not to go poking around! And. AND! The camp library went bonkers when I found that history book! It nearly killed us trying to destroy it!

It's like this—

Something at Camp Sweetwater wants us to listen—badly.

And something else *really* doesn't want us to.

So obviously, we're going to have to listen.

No matter what.

Corryn

The evening's activity is called a listening hike.

I like hiking. Am okay with listening. It's one of my five favorite senses. Definitely above smelling; smelling is really kind of stupid.

To begin the hike, all the cabins from Oak Camp meet on the path in front of the archery and rifle ranges. I didn't even know we had archery and rifle ranges. Whose idea was it to give these doofuses weapons?! Just the words *rifle range* give me the willies. I'm not a big fan of guns. I'm like Batman in that way (and many, many others we can discuss later).

Surrounded by Ew and Braids and Hairspray, I get a gander at the meet-up. It seems like the whole junior camp is gathered here, which makes it feel less like a hike and more like a parade. Someone should be on a unicycle up front, twirling a baton.

The warm, still night is filled with giggling and singing, not to mention the constant "hi-ya!" accompanying kung fu kicks.

Even the little ones are here, brave little campers clutching Cabbage Patch dolls and nervously flicking yo-yos. I overhear one junior counselor reminding their charges to be "gentle and kind," which I guess is another way to say, "don't shove the person in front of you just because you're losing your teeny little minds in the dark." The purpose of the hike, apparently, is to make us less afraid of said dark.

News flash: It's not the dark that hurts you. It's what hides in it.

Gavin and Scary Mary are here, lucky us, and it is Mary who explains the rules of the listening hike to us.

She reads from a piece of paper, so I have the strong feeling this is her first as well.

"Right, uh, listen," she says. "A listening hike is like a regular hike, but using only our eyes and ears. Using only our eyes and ears, we walk through the forest."

"We walk on our eyes and ears?" Nostrils cracks.

"Shut it," Gavin says.

Mary continues reading. "The best, uh, birders can identify a species without seeing a single feather. All they need is the sound."

"I can identify an owl," Nostrils says. "But for some reason they can't identify me."

"What are you talking about?" Gavin says.

"Owls can't identify me," Nostrils says. "They keep asking 'who?'"

"Of *course* they can't identify you, they're bloody owls, aren't they?!" Gavin barks.

It was a pretty good one by old Nostrils, but of course Gavin didn't get it. I'd call him a birdbrain but that would be mean to birds.

Mary continues. "No flashlights on this trip. We are going to walk in total darkness and note what we observe."

"I observe total darkness," Nostrils says. He's *on fire*, cracking up pretty much everyone. Tez does not seem to be enjoying the comedy show, however. I elbow him in the ribs.

"No flashlights, huh?" I say. "I guess they're trying to get rid of some of the little ones." No reaction. I elbow him again. "Good thing there are no wolves in Ohio, right, Tez?" Nothing.

One of the babies from baby camp burps really loud and Gavin barks out, "No noises!"

"That was a sound of nature, a real Carolina Barking Spider!" Nostrils says. Then he rips a huge burp of his own. *Brrrrrap!* "And that, my friends, was a bear."

This really sets off the giggles from the babies from camp baby for babies. I notice some of the girls in baby camp keep looking over at Tez, waving and trying to catch his eye.

"Is that your fan club over there?" I say, elbowing him again.

All he says is "Stop elbowing me."

I elbow him again.

Mary abandons her script; it's not like we care anyway. "Listen for birds or whatever. You know, robins. The red ones." Does she really not know what a cardinal is? And why is she leading us on a bird-watching expedition at night?

Tez can't let this one slide.

"Actually, robins are typically active during the day," he says.

"I wish your mouth was only active during the never!" Gavin replies. Harsh.

Tez really can't help himself. "*Early bird gets the worm* is not just an expression, you see. Robins and many other birds are diurnal, which means that—"

"Diarrhea, cha-cha-cha!" shouts one of Tez's pint-sized fan club.

"Not diarrhea, *diurnal*."

"Diarrhea," shouts a crowd of babies.

"Would you all shut your bloody mouths?!" Gavin is getting so angry that I think I can see smoke rising off his head in the moonlight. Tez shrugs. He looks kind of sad. As we start the hike into the gloomy dark of night, I elbow him one more time.

"Stop elbowing me!" Tez says, his voice echoing in the quiet as, for one brief moment, the entire group takes Mary's direction and zips their bloody lips.

"Hey, I know what kind of bird that is," Nostrils says. "A lovebird!"

Har, har, har. Nostrils is about to get a fat one, right in his lip. Next to me, Tez burns, his brows knit hard in the middle of his not insubstantial forehead. (It's not quite a fivehead, but it's getting there.)

"Dude, what is wrong?" I ask. "Don't listen to those idiots."

"I never do. I'm *thinking*. I'm trying to remember if I saw a library on the bus ride in," he says.

"Okaaay."

"And I can't remember what I saw because I was kind of distracted by your underwear."

"You? How do you think I felt?!" I elbow him again. "But underwear or not, there probably is a library. I mean, most towns have them. Theirs might not even be haunted!"

"Yeah," he says. "Most towns do. Even in Ohio. Now, how on Middle Earth are we going to get there?"

We're whispering now, speaking barely louder than the hushed crunch of dry grass beneath our feet. We don't want to draw any more ire from the Brits or oohs and aahs from the giggling chorus of babies.

"Why do we have to get to the town library?" I ask. It's a fair question, but I think I already know the answer.

"Someone has to figure out what's wrong with this haunted camp before more than a bowl cut gets exterminated," he says.

Just then an owl announces its question to the night. *Who? Who? Who?*

"Us," Tez says. "*We* have to."

"Okay," I say. "Meet me tomorrow after breakfast. I have a plan."

15
The Great Escape

June 10, 1983

Corryn

I'm supposed to be playing tennis after breakfast.

I'm concerned Örn, the tennis coach, will note my absence if I'm sneaking into the town library instead of losing forty-five million to love again.

I seriously hate tennis. What's love got to do with it? It's worse than bowling; at least with bowling, you get to eat pretzels.

"Come on, Tez," I say as we head out from breakfast. "I have to quick fake something so Örn doesn't wonder where I am."

"Who, or *what*, is an Örn?" he asks.

"The instructor. How do you not know this? Don't you have tennis?"

"No," he says. "I hate it. It's worse than bowling."

"That's what I was just thinking!" I'd marvel for a bit at our obvious psychic connection, but I'm determined not to be distracted. I demand, "How did you get out of tennis? What sport are you signed up for?"

"I'm a basketball star," he says. "Didn't you know? I'm like the Chamorro Larry Bird. *Hafa adai!*"

This makes me laugh. Larry Bird? But Tez is so . . . slow!

Maybe a huge transformation comes over him when he sets foot on the hardwood. I don't want to be rude. "Oh," I say. "That's . . ."

"Just kidding," he says. "I didn't sign up for any sports."

"I thought sports were mandatory?"

He just shrugs. "Mandatory shmandatory." Seems like Tez has a little bit of a rule-breaker in him. A little rebel. I like it. It could come in handy.

"Okay," I say. "When we get close to the tennis courts, I'm going to have to put my arm around you."

"Your what? Around my who?"

"Relax, Tez," I say. "Just to pretend I sprained my

ankle. Örn will totally fall for it. I'll say you're taking me to the infirmary. He's not very smart."

"Yeah, you don't usually choose a career in the high-stakes world of summer-camp tennis if rocket science is also on the table. But . . . it's just that . . ." He gulps.

"You okay, Chamorro Larry Bird? Can't lose your nerve now."

"I'm fine," he says. "Totally cool as a . . . cool guy. Just, um, do we have to actually go to the infirmary? Because I really don't want to go back there. Miss Kortepeter scares the heck out me, with her beady eyes and habit of morphing into a blood demon."

"Keep up, Tez." I bark the words at him. "We're just *pretending* to go to the infirmary."

"Oh. Got it," he says. He looks visibly relieved.

We turn the corner on the main path and see the tennis courts up ahead. Örn is barking commands and delivering stinging backhands. I throw my arm around Tez's shoulder and whisper, "Okay. Acting!" I start to limp, first on my left foot, then my right. I lean into him and he supports my weight rather easily. He's surprisingly strong.

"Pick a foot," he whispers.

"Okay, right, sorry." I commit to the right-foot limp. I've hurt myself a lot of times riding BMX. I can channel an effective limp pretty easily, I'm guessing. Usually I'm trying to downplay the injury so Mom and Dad don't get nervous and threaten to take Elliot away, but playing up an injury is well within my range.

Tez leads me to the tennis courts. Örn is engrossed in screaming at Braids about her subpar serving technique. She looks mortified. Tez coughs to try to get Örn's attention. Örn does not seem to notice. Subtlety does not seem to be working.

I scream out, "Ow!"

Örn turns his sweaty head in our direction. "There you are," he says. "Quit monkeying around and pick up a racket. We really need to go over your—"

"Sorry, Örn," I say. "Can't today. I really hurt my ankle. Can't hardly stand." I point to my foot. I realize I point to the wrong one, but he doesn't seem to notice.

"Okay then," he says. "Well, there are plenty of racket skills you can practice while sitting down."

I wince. "Oooh, no, it's really bad. I have to go to the infirmary."

"Who are you?" Örn yells, pointing with his racket at Tez. "Why haven't I seen you on my courts before?"

"I, uh, um, Larry Bird!" Tez yells. Smooth. Effective though.

Örn rolls his eyes, adjusts his headband, scoops a tennis ball off the ground with his racket, and fires it toward a group of tennis players lollygagging against the fence.

"Book it!" Tez whispers.

"Injured, remember?" I say, but he bolts. Sort of.

Hilariously, Tez's version of booking is just walking really fast. He looks like one of those windup drum monkeys, and I'm trying not to howl with laughter. With a quick look behind me, I realize Örn is back in tennis mode. I could probably cartwheel after Tez to catch up and he wouldn't notice. But instead I laugh and break into a sprint.

"Wait up!" I say, like I can't catch up with three long strides.

I hope Tez knows where he's going, because I'm sure following him.

I mean, he should know the way. He's memorized the *Camper's Guidebook*, apparently. And hey, it turns out he delivers! The parking lot isn't too far from the infirmary, which is convenient in case anyone sees me.

The original sprained ankle story holds up. The sprinting might be hard to explain, but we'll get there when we get there.

Tez leans against the Director's Lodge, panting. Man, he's out of shape. His monkey walk was barely faster than a regular walk.

"Look," he says, pointing. "Camp van."

Indeed, the Camp Sweetwater van idles loudly in the parking lot. It's presumably preparing to take off on a voyage into town. We just have to figure out how to get on board.

I remember some pictures in one of my BMX magazines that showed pro skateboarders "hitchhiking" on the back of a truck. They'd grab the bumper and go for a free ride. Seems really fun. Too bad we don't have skateboards.

"We'll have to get in the back without being seen," I say.

"Easier said than done," he replies, which is putting it somewhat mildly.

"Most things are," I say. "Except selling seashells at the seashore."

"What?"

"Sorry. That's something my dad says."

We peek around the office wall and scan the parking lot. There is a lot of activity, counselors and other camp staff milling around, cars coming and going. It seems impossible to get into the van without being seen.

"Maybe I can create a diversion," Tez says. "I'm already the guy who chunders. Old Pukeface McChickenlips. I could start screaming, then make myself barf, and then you could sprint into the van. At least one of us would get to go to town."

"No way," I say. "We're doing this as a team or we're not doing this at all. And I think I know just the way to do it . . ."

Stuffed under a tarp, Tez and I rock back and forth in the cargo hold of the van.

It turns out that offering to help load the empty milk crates into the shuttle gives a couple of stowaways access to the shuttle. One brief, easy chore later, we're on our way to town with nobody the wiser.

"We're getting away with this," Tez whispers. Clutching his knees to his chest, he grins like a loon. He's way too happy to be crammed under a mildewy tarp. "This is totally working."

Okay. I kind of can't help grinning back. "We jumped the turnstile."

"We dodged our fare."

"We nicked our ticket," I say, doing my best Mary impression.

"Pardon me, madame," Tez says, joining me in pretending to be bloody British. "I absolutely cannot have any fare dodging on our horseless carriage."

"Avast! Ye gods! Cheerio!" I whisper back.

Tez has to bury a couple of giggles before he manages to squeak out, "Bless my figgy pudding, there's been a ticket nicking!"

I clap a hand over my mouth. That's the stupidest, funniest thing I've ever heard. And trying not to laugh makes it so much funnier, like when someone farts in church.

Tez presses his face to his knees to keep from laughing out loud. A bunch of counselors sit in the seat just a few feet from us. Scary Mary yaps at top volume to some guy named Chip, who sounds like he got poured out of a private school and right into a regatta. Right now, Mary's telling him the best places to hide in the woods in order to smoke and . . . stuff. The *stuff* sounds kind of sleazy.

As soon as I get my breath under control, I part my fingers and whisper back to Tez, "I say, this is a *dastardly* ticket nicking! A *wicked* nicking!"

"A nick-nack paddy wicking?" he chokes. Then Tez hides his whole head to bury his laughter.

And that's how we get to town: rattling around with empty milk crates, under a tarp, laughing in stupid British accents while we hitch a secret ride.

Sometimes, camp is pretty awesome.

16
Fondue Lock

Corryn

After a long, hot, stinky—did I mention long?—ride to town, the van finally rumbles to a stop. Tez and I listen for the doors to slam shut and the voices to fade away. Finally, there is relative quiet—just the occasional car passing by.

"Let's go," I say. I start to pull the tarp off.

"Wait," he whispers, pulling it back down. "I counted an odd number of doors."

"You're an odd counter of doors," I whisper.

"I'm guessing someone is either still in the van or they left one of the doors open," he says. "Someone might be heading back or still here. Just be patient."

"It's hard to be patient in this cloud of farts," I whisper.

"I also counted an odd number of farts," he says. "And I only fart even numbers."

I start to laugh, but then I hear another door slam. Tez was right! One of the counselors was taking their sweet time getting out of the van. I can't believe we haven't been caught. We wait another minute to make sure the coast is clear and then rip off the tarp.

We climb out of the cargo hold and pop open the door. The air smells sweet and oily, like hot asphalt. Tez and I both stretch our arms up to the sunny sky and breathe deeply. We sigh in unison. It's like we're exact mirrors of one another. We both start giggling.

This giggling has got to stop. We have work to do!

Tez closes the back door of the van, careful to make sure it doesn't latch. He gives me a knowing look. We will need that door to stay open so we can sneak back in for the return to camp. I nod knowingly back at him and wink.

"I figure we have at least two hours," he says. "Better to be back early than left behind! Say, now, what have you got for us, Fan du Lac?"

“Fan du Lac?” I repeat. “What’s that?” I start giggling again. My dad would say I’ve been out in the giggleweeds. Now that I think about it, my dad says a lot of weird stuff, in between the bad jokes that dads tell (like, did you hear about the guy who stole a calendar? He got twelve months. Ba da dum).

“Fan du Lac is the name of the town.” Tez just blinks at me.

“Pretty funny name, right?” I laugh. “Makes me think of cheese. Fondue lock.”

Tez grabs me by the hand and shouts, “Duck!” so I do. The expression on his face becomes one of panic.

Well, that’ll mow down the giggleweeds.

Crouched behind the van, I whisper, “What?” My hands start to sweat and my heart starts to race.

“I think that’s one of the counselors from senior camp,” he whispers, gesturing toward the suspicious individual with his head.

“So what?” I say.

“If she sees us, we’re busted.”

After a moment, we rise slowly and scan the street, carefully looking for any signs of Sweetwater counselors. There are none. We start to walk, each in opposite directions. We realize we have no idea where we're going. We're on what I guess is the main street of Fan du Lac.

It's a fairly typical small-town main street, with various shops and restaurants. There are shoppers milling about. There is a fairly large restaurant called Pancake Hut (spelled *Pan ake Hu* on the sign). That's the place Scary Mary mentioned. We definitely need to stay away from there.

"If *you* were a library, where would *you* be?" Tez says.

We head down the street, away from the Hut. There are no signs of a library, but I do see a policeman. My instinct is to turn and run. I've never been AWOL before. Never been on the run. On top of that, we're fare dodgers! If we're caught, we'll be hauled into the clink!

Naturally, that means Tez marches right up to the policeman.

I'm frozen. What is he doing? The cop's not particularly friendly looking. He's tall, with a long neck and long arms. His uniform doesn't seem to fit him all that well. His mustache looks like it was drawn on with a thick marker, two dark black lines angling down from his top lip. Talk about dastardly.

"Hi, hi, uh, hello Officer . . . Wolpaw," Tez says, reading his name tag in a really obvious way.

"You aren't gonna be from around here, will you be then?"

Whoa, what's up with that? I feel a lump in my throat. Is that a comment about Tez's skin color? Was there a report filed from camp already? Or is this small-town officer about to pull some sort of Sherlock Holmes move, where he knows everything about us based on a quick glance?

"Um, well, no, actually, we're on vacation, you see . . . ," Tez says.

"Not from the camp?"

Tez almost breaks his neck shaking his head. "Nooo. We're here with responsible adults. On *vacation*."

"How did you know that we're not from here?" I ask, veering the subject to safety. Also, I narrow my eyes and stick out my chest, to let him know that I won't be party to his discriminatory attitude.

Wolpaw smiles. "All the kids around here know me as *Chief* Wolpaw," he says, tipping his cap. He winks and smiles, which has the effect of making his mustache appear somewhat less dastardly.

"Oh," I say. "Right."

"What can the chief of police do for you vacationers?"

"We're looking for the library!" Tez says with way too much enthusiasm.

"Not what I expected from a couple of kids on a beautiful day like today, but okay," says Wolpaw. "It's not far from here at all. You must have walked right past it. Go back the way you came, and it's almost to the corner. I'd say you can't miss it, but . . ."

"Thanks!" we say in unison. I turn to follow his directions. I'm hecka glad that he didn't bust us and really happy that he has pointed us in the right direction. I'm anxious to get moving but notice Tez isn't walking next to me. I turn around to see him continuing his conversation with Chief Wolpaw.

"One more thing," Tez says. "It's been bothering me. Do you happen to know what the name of the town means? Fan du Lac?"

"Good question," Chief Wolpaw says with a smile. "It's from the French. Somewhere along the way it was shortened from *Fantôme du Lac. Lac* means lake, as you mighta guessed. *Fantôme* is the French word for . . ."

Tez finishes his sentence for him. "Ghost."

Fantôme du Lac.

Ghost of the lake.

In case we needed one more bit of evidence that this place is mega, super, ultra-extra haunted. With super-natural sauce on top.

Tez

The clown magician in the library is entirely too happy to see us. I sort of feel like I should stand between him and Corryn, to protect *him*. She's got danger in her eyes, and I've seen Corryn square off. She knows some deadly moves, and Sketchy the Clown isn't prepared.

"Come on in, come on in," the clown says, pulling silk flowers out of the secret panel sewn into his sleeve. "The show's about to start!"

Plainly, he has no idea how much danger he's in. Before Corryn takes him out, I shake my head politely. "We're here to do some research, but thanks anyway."

As Corryn and I peel away from him, she mutters, "Clowns in the library? There really is something wrong with this place."

Pointing at a Summer Reading sign, I say, "Carnival of Books. It's a theme."

Corryn shoots me a look. "It's a creepy theme."

We glance back at the clown magician. All I see is a paunchy, middle-aged man in greasepaint, doing tricks from a book he probably picked up in the 790s (assuming that the Fan du Lac library subscribes to the Dewey Decimal system). I don't find him creepy. A little sad, maybe.

Okay, a little sad definitely.

We walk up to the librarian's desk. The nameplate says "Mr. Ferdle," and the librarian behind the nameplate is another middle-aged man. He looks up at us expectantly, his black and gray goatee practically quivering.

"Can I help you?"

Corryn and I both start to talk at once. After a second, I shut up, because Corryn's definitely not going to uncle out first. She bends her fingers back on the edge of the desk, leaning forward almost eagerly.

"We want everything you have on Camp Sweetwater, 1883. The"—she searches for the right word—"disappearances."

Mr. Ferdle hesitates, then nods. "It's all on microfilm, and there's really not a lot. It was a long time ago, and they never found those poor girls."

Bingo.

"But! We just received several copies of the brand-new *Au Pairs Association* book. It's a very popular series. Especially for girls. Perhaps you'd like to be the first to—"

"*The microfilm.*" Corryn sets her shoulders. "We'd like to see what you have."

With an air of disappointment, Mr. Ferdle gets up from the desk and leads us into a stuffy room in the back of the library.

Wide screens fill up a bench on one side, and there are shelves with marked cartridges filling the rest. Mr. Ferdle doesn't even have to look. He pulls out a few cartridges almost by rote and loads them into the microfilm machine.

The dizzying spin of microfilm stories whooshing by on-screen makes me a little seasick, but neither Corryn nor I take our eyes from the screens. A spin of the dial, and *whirrrl*, Victorian stuff all over the place, and man, the prices were crazy. They have solid-gold watch chains for a dollar fifty, and a brand-new road buggy, forty-seven dollars even. I commit those numbers to memory. You never know when that kind of information might become useful.

There's one article, not even on the front of the

paper. “Inquiry into Terrible Camping-Ground Horror.” Great title, but it doesn’t say much at all; big surprise, it goes on about how the local constable and various *gentlemen* had a meeting to talk about the (unnamed) horror. It doesn’t even name the girls.

Fortunately, another article does. “What Has Become of the Benighted Sweetwater Three?” Again, 1880s reporting pretty much just repeats the title of the article in the text, but we do confirm something useful: their names were Virginia Finch, Leigh Wade, and Dorothy Duane.

I show Corryn, and then jot the names down. It’s interesting, but we have a lot of ground to cover. We scroll on, the machines getting hot as we spin away. There are a few more repeat articles, and it’s just weird. They’re all written like everybody in Fan du Lac already knows the details, which means the paper doesn’t have to get into them. It’s like these articles are whispering, gossiping instead of reporting. After two more reels, it doesn’t seem to get better. Time to try something else.

Murmuring to Corryn, I say, “Let’s go see if there’s any local history books. Or folklore. Maybe they’ll tell us something.”

"I thought you were all about the data," Corryn asks, raising a brow at me.

"There's always a little truth in local legends."

Abandoning the microfilm, we skirt past the creepy clown magician, who is currently pouring milk into a plastic bottle hidden in a giant silk hat. The kids sitting on the floor around him are loving this. I decide not to ruin the wonder for them, even though it's fairly obvious how all of it works.

The local history section is pretty thin. Most of the books look like they were published in somebody's basement. But that's okay—we want *actual* local legends, not the stories that random outsiders write. I start at one end of the shelf, and Corryn works her way down the other.

"*Plows of Sweetwater County*," Corryn says skeptically.

I offer up in return, "*A Pictorial History of the Doors and Windows of Fan du Lac*."

Corryn snorts. "That's probably it. One of the historical doors at camp is possessed."

"Haaaaunted doooooor," I whisper, and we both laugh. Scanning down the shelves, nothing jumps out at me. Not until the very bottom shelf anyway. Squinting,

I reread the title, because I'm not completely sure of what I'm seeing. But I didn't imagine it, not even a little.

Pulling a slender volume from the shelf, I shiver—the same cold, uneasy shiver I felt when we watched the fire come to life. I clear my throat, thumbing through the table of contents, and then show the cover to Corryn. "Uh, I think I found something."

She starts to say "What?" but cuts herself off at the *Wh*. The title says it all for both of us.

MECHANT'S CURSE AND THE FIGHT FOR FAN DU LAC'S SOUL

17
Legend Has It

Tez

"Okay, that's basically all of them," Corryn says, sliding into the seat next to me.

She's liberated a bunch of slips of paper from the card catalog tables, and six or seven tiny pencils as well. While planning our escape from camp, we failed to plan for data collection.

We had no pens, no pads of paper, and no dimes for the Xerox machine. There was no way I was stealing a book from the library, and Mr. Ferdle said we'd need our parents to come in to get us a summer guest card.

Instead, we have about a thousand tiny rectangles of

paper. We perch ourselves by the window in the baby area. We probably look out of place surrounded by picture books and block puzzles, but we can see Pancake Hut (*Pan ake Hu*) from here—and more important, the shuttle van back to camp.

"All right," I say, paraphrasing as fast as I can. "The first chapter says in the late 1600s, the Miami nation of Native Americans had settlements near the lake. But French fur trappers showed up in the early 1700s, and they were sort of friendly. But all of a sudden in 1732, the Miami abandoned the lake."

Corryn scribbles across a reference slip, then another. "Why, though?"

Pointing at the page, I tell her, "Because this French guy, Arnaud Mechant, cursed the lake. I mean, I doubt that's how the Miami peoples put it, since they have a completely different theological system than Europeans. . . ."

"Stay on target, Tez," Corryn warns.

"I'm just saying, they said he personally *put something in the lake to ruin it.*"

Elbowing into me, Corryn turns the book to look at it. She skims pages as fast as I do, and that gives me a chance to glance at the shuttle. Still there. All good.

Corryn knots a hand in her hair and sort of boggles at the page. "We know this story."

For a second, I think maybe she's read the book before. But then I remember. "Nostrils! In the Great Hall! With the vampire devils!"

"I thought it was just a ghost story."

"We're kind of living in a ghost story," I point out.

Corryn thinks about this for a minute. "So, like, there have been a lot of disappearances and murders, but I think this author might be a little loopty-loop."

"Did the title give it away?"

"He's totally serious about the vampire devils." Corryn clears her throat, then starts to read. "Legend has it that Mechant and his family were driven out of France and into the New World. A coarse and ugly family legacy of violence dogged him to what would become our fair town of Fan du Lac. Of course, many believe there's truth in the strange tales of double-hearted vampire devils following him here—literally."

Despite everything we've seen the last couple of days, I snort. A little. There's nothing wrong with healthy skepticism, and come on. Sarcastic, I say, "Everyone familiar with vampire lore knows vampires can't cross running water *or* salt water."

"Don't fight with me," Corryn says. "Fight with the book. And look. Newspaper clippings about a dude who actually murdered somebody to feed blood to the vampire devils in the lake."

"You lie."

"I don't!"

Pulling the book to me, I read it for myself. Some creepy dude in the forties actually broke into his neighbor's house, chopped the neighbor up, then waited on the blood-soaked bed for the cops to arrive. When they did, they asked him why and all the dude said was that he had to "feed the lake."

I flick through the pages, and there's a timeline of disappearances or bloody deaths, on a fairly regular basis.

It turns out that there's a cycle. The camp opens for a while. People disappear, and the camp closes. Then wait twenty years, the camp opens for a while, people disappear, and then guess what? It closes again!

Most of the time, I believe that things like this are a coincidence, but this is the creepiest coincidence I've ever seen.

The pit of my stomach squiggles with something unpleasant. I flick the pages, reading bits and pieces for

Corryn. It turns out those black, gnarly sticks we found are from an unusual species of oak tree that used to grow around here. There was a massive one right next to the lake. The locals called it devilwood, and it exploded into a million pieces when lightning hit it in the 1940s.

When the government put in the local highway, construction workers kept having horrible accidents—falling into cement and drowning, or having giant beams drop on them. In the fifties, most of the old camp burned down and had to be rebuilt. Apparently, Primrose is one of the few original sections left from the 1800s.

Finally, we discover that Mechant had a hunting lodge near the lake, but he, his family, and the lodge disappeared off the face of the earth. I share all of this with Corryn, along with an observation:

"Exactly the place you should build a summer camp."

"It is if you hate your kids," Corryn says. She sounds a little bitter.

I'm not sure how much time we have left. I flip to the shiny pages in the middle with pictures. Sometimes they really are worth a thousand words. Sometimes they leave you speechless.

There's an aerial photo of Fan du Lac and Camp Sweetwater, with the lake right in the middle of camp.

Somebody marked white dots where deaths or disappearances occurred. They ring right around the lake, never straying too far from its shores. Just bodies and disappearances, and disappearances and bodies. Way too many for this small of a place.

And it's kind of weird, but from overhead, the lake looks . . . well, sort of like a head. With horns on it.

Devil horns.

"Oh my God," Corryn yelps, and I nearly fall out of my chair. Did she read my mind?! But no, she's pointing over my shoulder at the window we haven't been checking.

I look in the direction she's indicating and make a horrifying discovery: either Noodles the Magician is talented enough to make a shuttle van disappear . . .

Or we just got left in town.

Corryn

I'm! Freaking! Out!

The parking space near Pancake Hut, where once sat a very large white van, is now filled with a medium-sized green car. (I think it is a Chrysler LeBaron.) I feel my eyes go huge. I can't even talk. I point out the window with one hand and punch Tez with the other.

"Ow!" he says. "What the—?!"

I point again.

"I know!" he says.

"We're toast," I say through gritted teeth.

Weirdo the Magician does something apparently hilarious, like pulling a rabbit out of his left armpit, because the collected rug rats in the j section of the library erupt in a roar of laughter. It feels like they are mocking us. *Shut up, summer reading club participants of Fan du Lac!*

"Chrysler LeBaron," Tez says, making it sound like a swear. He tugs at his hair and whistles on the inhale. "This is not good."

"You think?" I say. "Forget about Fan du Lac's soul—we need to worry about our own rear ends."

"Come on," he says, hopping up and gathering all our notes like he's a blackjack dealer and someone just busted.

I don't know how on earth he thinks we're going to catch a van driven by a teenager all hopped up on maple syrup, but it beats sitting here being mocked by the Easily Amused Ankle Biters Society.

In about two seconds, Tez has stuffed all our notes

into his pockets and is up and out the door. A few pieces of paper fly out of his pockets, trailing behind him like the plumage of a panicked bird. I snatch them up as I rush after him.

We're through the door and out of the quiet coolness of the Fan du Lac library into what has become a scorcher of a day. The noises of summer are all around—birds chirping and children laughing and the far-off jingle-jangle of an ice cream truck.

Out on Main Street, we whip our heads around frantically. We're desperately hoping to see someone from camp but also terrified of being caught.

"What are we going to do?" we both say at the same exact moment. I guess that answers that question. He doesn't know either. We're sunk.

"Should we just start walking?" he says.

"I have no idea which way to go," I say.

"What about the metal in your nose?" he asks, deadpan. Is this goofus making a joke?

I say, "Iron in my beak—"

"Yes. That."

"I have a good sense of direction," I say. "But I don't think it works when you can't even see where you're going. We were stuck under a tarp, if you remember."

"Oh, I remember," he says. "And now we're totally toast."

"Everything from A to Z can be found at the library," I say, pointing behind me with my thumb. It's something my librarian from school, Mrs. Gratsky, used to say. I don't think she meant it like, everything including how to get back to the camp you snuck out of and which you need to get back to even though there are vampire devils there. But, you know, she's not wrong.

"I guess we could ask for a map of the area," Tez says. "That seems like the kind of thing the library might—"

My heart is pounding and I don't feel like waiting. I turn right around and head back into the library. Tez hustles in behind me.

Cloppy the Magician has apparently completed his act. I don't know if he cut himself in half or turned into a rabbit and hopped right away, but he's gone. There's a sea of small children running rampant now. We have to wade through them and maybe hip-check a few to get up to the desk.

We are waiting in an endless line. With each tick of the clock I feel my heart drop lower in my chest. Click, click, click. Thump, thump, thump.

Finally, it's our turn with the librarian. There's a

small opening between two kids and I pounce. "Which direction is Camp Sweetwater?" I blurt out.

Ferdle narrows his eyes and peers out at me over his spectacles. "I thought you were on vacation."

"Yes, well, I mean, we are, but we are *quite* interested in seeing the local landmarks and regional—" Tez is a lot of things but he is not a good liar.

The librarian cuts him off with a dismissive wave. There is a crushing throng of eager readers behind us who will apparently die if they don't get their cards stamped, and Ferdle doesn't have time for our shenanigans. He hands us a map.

"Just take it," he says.

Tez snatches the map and we're out the door. We're back on the street, sweating in the hot sun. He keeps rubbing his chest as he turns around, eyeing our surroundings. "Now," he says, looking up at the sky, "if we orient ourselves to the east this-a-way . . ."

"You're holding the map upside down," I say. He isn't, but I felt like saying it.

"Ha ha. Funny with the jokes over here. How are you not scared out of your mind?" he asks.

"I am!"

"Weird way of showing it."

"I know! I'm sorry!"

"What will happen if we get caught sneaking into town?" he says.

"Isn't it in the handbook?" I ask.

"It's not, but it can't be good. They'll probably kick us out of camp! They'll send us home!"

Oh God. Plunked right back into the middle of divorce carnage? "I don't want that!" I say.

"I don't either!" he says. Then he pauses. "What's wrong with us that we don't want to leave what is very clearly a haunted camp? Most people would be begging to leave."

"Most people aren't us," I say with a shrug. "We're like firefighters. When others run away, we run in."

"We are totally going to save Camp Sweetwater," he says, patting the puffy clumps of notes in his pocket.

"*If* we don't get kicked out first." I say. "*If* we can figure out how on earth to get back there."

"It's the beads, isn't it?" he teases. "You can't bear to lose any."

"Duh, obviously." I say. "Beads are my life . . . But I kinda also don't hate hanging out with you. And, I mean . . . on top of which, I don't even know if I have a house to go home to anymore."

Neither of us say anything after that. It's awkward, but not in a bad way. I shuffle around, looking everywhere but at Tez. And that turns out to be a good thing. My eyes land on the solution to all our problems.

Leaning up against a tree outside the library is the answer to our wishes. It's no Elliot. Not a BMX racing bike. Not by a long shot. It's a tandem bike. That's right: a bicycle built for two. Only problem is we'd have to steal it.

"Too bad we can't, you know . . . borrow this here sweet ride." I tap the seat.

"Borrow it? Are you nuts? Borrowing implies returning. How could we possibly return it? What you're talking about is stealing. Need I remind you that the chief of police could be lurking anywhere around here? We already lied to him once."

"Somehow, I don't think it's a felony to impersonate a vacationer, diaper baby. Very smooth, by the way. *Nooo, Chief Wolpaw. We're here with responsible adults. On a responsible vacation to be responsible.*"

There is a long pause. "You don't have to make fun of me," he says. Like, he has tears in his eyes and everything.

"What? No, I'm sorry," I say. "It was quick thinking.

And brave to go right up to Wolpaw. I wanted to book it as soon as I saw him."

"I meant the diaper baby part," Tez says.

"Oh." Really? That's what set him off? Tez is a weirdo, but he's kind of my weirdo. I don't want him to feel bad. The diaper baby thing isn't a thing. I just . . . said it. Maybe I shouldn't have. I put a hand on his shoulder and say, "Okay. It's banned forever."

"Thanks," Tez says, and offers a smile.

"I'll take the heat on this one. We get busted with the bike, I'll say it was my idea. One hundred percent. Dragged you along against your wishes. Deal?" I say.

"Well, I guess if we do make an effort to return it . . . I think the owner will understand that we are really under extreme duress here."

"Oh, so extreme, the duress."

"Okay, deal," he says, extending his hand to shake mine.

While our hands are moving toward each other to seal the deal, I slip in one more detail. Using my best super-fast-talker-auctioneer voice, I add, "I call front seat, no callbacks!"

It feels amazing to be back on a bike. This tandem is slow and clunky, and its handlebars are seriously borked. Plus, there's about a hundred pounds of Tez slapped on the back, dragging me down. Theoretically having a second rider would increase your pedal power. Theoretically.

Riding a tandem bike is actually pretty hard. We had lots of false starts and nearly bailed about a hundred times before we got the hang of it. The trip back to camp is essentially a straight shot. Unfortunately, it's also essentially straight up. It's not quite what you'd call a mountain, but it's definitely a quad burner.

The sky roars. A boom of thunder so loud you can't call it a clap. More like a roar—a thunderroar. A blinding flash of lightning, then a ripping boom like the ground being torn in two. Oh no! Something is happening again. Evil unleashed? Demon clouds? Fiery hellstones? Raindrops of blood?

The thunder roars again. Nope. It's just a summer storm. Just a regular Ohio summer storm. Just raindrops made of rain. It has nothing to do with cursed souls, vampire devils, or screaming ghosts.

I think.

18
Camp Devilwood

Tez

After we stash the bike in the woods, Corryn and I slip back into camp like we never left.

First, we hit our cabins and get into something dry. Then we have to figure out what time it is with no watch and no sun. Since everything seems kind of deserted in Oak Camp, we finally decide it must be about lunchtime. And if not, we'll probably find everybody else on our way to the Great Hall.

It's still raining, and there's nobody at the lake. The water churns, frothy and white. There are shadows on it, and there shouldn't be. The sky is pretty uniformly gray on gray on gray. It's like the water's alive . . . or undead, given what we read about this place.

We reach the Great Hall, and we both shudder when Scary Mary's voice booms between the thunder overheard.

"Oi, the little lovebirds are last again," she caws. "Bet I know what they were up to, besides losing beads for their cabins!"

Gavin laughs and pretends to kiss the back of his hand. Bowl Cut rolls his eyes at him, and Ew tells Corryn, "They're dweebs. Just ignore them."

"Thanks," Corryn mumbles.

Then Bowl Cut and Ew let us cut in line. Huh. Are they our . . . friends?

After we get our grilled cheese and soup, Corryn and I take one of the middle tables. Scary Mary and Gavin always skitter around the edges to sneak out. Directly beneath the big wood wagon-wheel chandelier is the safest place to be for us.

When Hairspray ventures close, Corryn clears her throat and says, "Is that a bug?" Hairspray turns on her heel and bails for the other side of the room.

"All right," Corryn says decisively. "We need a plan."

Unfortunately, she looks at me like I should have

one. And I don't. I just don't. Tearing my sandwich in half, I hedge, "I have to wait for the notes to dry out to really . . ."

Corryn picks a piece of dried cheese off the side of her sandwich and flicks it into my soup. "We agreed, right? There's something bad going on and we're the only ones who can do something about it."

I fish the cheese out of my soup with the back of my spoon. "We did. And we are. But we can't just do *some*thing; we have to do *the* thing. And we don't know enough to figure out what that is."

With a frown, Corryn puts her sandwich down. It's actually possible to set a sandwich aside in anger. Who knew?

"We're going to pretend like everything in that book that you found is true and go from there."

I don't know why I'm hesitating. But, I mean, obviously, I am. There's a quivery, uneasy feeling in my gut and my skin just feels different in camp. Like there's heat in the air that might turn into a wildfire at any minute. Back in town, everything was fine. I felt fine there—good, even. Brave. Now I want to hide in my cabin and wait for the storm, and the summer, to pass.

All at once, it hits me. I'm not afraid in town because

town doesn't want me to be afraid. But Camp Sweetwater . . . or whatever Mechant put in the bottom of the lake . . . does.

In spite of the squirming, worming nastiness in my belly, I sit up straighter. I'm going to make myself be brave. Corryn is counting on me.

"If we're assuming that everything in the book is true, then I think we can make *some* subsidiary assumptions."

"Oh, hi, Tez!" Corryn says, brightly sarcastic. "I'm glad you showed up! There was this total weenie pretending to be you—"

"Anyway," I say, interrupting her. My brain is on a roll, and I don't want my thoughts to get away. "It seems like there are two things happening here. One, the screaming faces. Scary as all get out, but they don't do anything."

"Which leads to two—" she starts.

"—the thing that's actually hurting people," I finish.

"The vampire devils?" Corryn supplies.

I make a face and shrug. "Sure, let's call it vampire devils."

"Go ahead," she says.

"Okay, the vampire devils, for lack of a better term,

are what's in the lake, and inside Miss Kortepeter, and what made Bowl Cut cut his hair and almost twisted Ew's head off. They might even be behind the bugs."

Corryn hesitates with a shudder, then takes a bite of her sandwich. "Okay. Agree. Go on."

"I think it's fair to say that the 'vampire devils' are responsible for the disappearing campers," I tell her. "Especially since they basically told us so."

"When?" Corryn asks. "A lot of weird stuff has happened, but we didn't get a candy gram with monster motives on it."

"The visions in the fire—those missing girls. They tried to show us what happened, so we would help them. But then Ew twisted her head half off and told you she *wants blood*. Not Ew personally. But the bad thing! It's hungry and it wants blood. Which means . . ."

Now Corryn gets it. She lights right up and fills in, "The bad thing. It ate the campers that went missing!"

"You saw the newspaper! It seems like they barely looked for them. Those girls may still be out there. Their bodies anyway."

The breath whooshes out of Corryn. "They never got to go home from camp."

I point at her. "Exactly. According to folklore, spirits

have earthly business that they left unsettled. What if the three campers in the fire aren't trying to scare us? What if they just want to go home?"

Pulling her bowl toward her, Corryn gazes into it for a moment. Then she looks up. "That's a problem, then. Because if their bodies are in the lake, we'll never get them back."

Finally, I'm relieved to be able to lay down some actual science. "If their bodies were in the lake, they would have found them a hundred years ago. They would've floated. The lake's not that big. I can see the other side from here."

Now Corryn pushes her soup, with all the alphabet letters floating in a bloody, tomato-y broth, away.

To distract her, I go on. "The book said Mechant had a hunting lodge, right? The one he built before he drove the Miami peoples away. Since he's the one who brought the 'vampire devils' to Lake Sweetwater, and since he's the one local history blames for cursing the land, I think we should start there. With his house."

"But it's gone," Corryn points out. "Two hundred years gone."

I shrug. "Maybe there's something left. Or maybe

there's not. But the place where it all started seems like a good place to start."

"There were old maps in those boxes at Primrose Camp," Corryn says, warming to the idea.

"Then we need to get them."

I don't point out, although I think Corryn will be totally into it, that this means breaking into the camp office to get them. That's where Gavin and Scary Mary were supposed to take the save pile after we cleared out the shed.

Once we can get at the maps, we can compare the ones we drew on reference slips to the official one. That will give us an idea of where to look for Mechant's original lodge site.

At least, I think it will. I hope.

Also? I'm stoked that I get to find out if reading about picking locks actually prepares you to do it.

Corryn

So, it turns out Tez can pick a lock.

He is pretty fine with what I guess the police would call "breaking and entering." It's kind of surprising, given how reluctant he was to swipe a bike. Oh no, have I turned sweet Tez to a life of crime? Well, desperate times call for desperate measures.

To get into the locked office, all he needed was a couple of bobby pins. I don't wear them, but I do share a bathroom with about eight hundred girls, so it wasn't hard to locate one.

I deliver the pins to Tez and we meet down at the camp office under the cover of darkness. He's like, "I've only read about this, never done it in practice . . ." He straightens the bobby pins and jiggles them in the lock for a second. Before I can doubt him too much, *pop!* The door creaks open.

The office looks like a bomb went off. A bomb full of old boxes, piles of paper, and stacks of CAMP SWEETWATER T-shirts. There are file cabinets and boxes overflowing with newspapers, mimeographed camp schedules, and calendars for a bunch of different years—just not this one.

This is probably what it looks like inside a time capsule. We buried one at my school last year. The people of the future are gonna be astounded by the Duran Duran tapes and copies of *Time* magazine with

David Bowie on the cover. (They *will* love, not sarcastically, my copy of *BMX Racer*.)

"Tez," I whisper.

He spins with his lantern, casting gloomy shadows on the office walls. "This filing system is terrible," he says. "None of these cabinets have any sort of labels on them. What we need is an original map."

I'm about to say something, but as he turns to face me, his lantern throws a bright beam onto the wall behind him.

"Gawp gawp," I say, and point. There, on the wall behind him, is a framed map.

"Oh yeah," he says, like he's been in here before. Has he?? Why?? Tez turns to inspect it.

It's huge, about three feet wide, and hung in a heavy wooden frame. It's not even level on the wall. It's about six bubbles off plumb, my dad would say. "How are we going to—" I start, but Tez is already is leaping up onto the desk, hoisting the heavy frame off its nail.

Wow! I really *have* turned Tez to a life of straight-up crime. I'd be proud if I weren't so nervous.

I peek out the windows of the office, into the deep darkness of camp at night, ever fearful that Scary Mary, or Gavin, or something worse will be lurking out there. The staff cabins are just across the way too. It's quiet though, save the sound of Tez's nervous whistling.

"Now, to put this in my pocket," Tez says with a laugh.

It's a pretty funny sight, seeing him try to stuff a yard-long picture frame into his tiny shorts' pocket. He's really enjoying this gag, pretending to stuff the frame in. Seriously though, how are we going to get it out of here?

Then the weight of the frame starts to pull his shorts down. I see a look of panic flash on his face before he reaches down to grab his waistband. With both hands. Which means that zero hands remain to hold the picture frame.

Gravity does its thing, and the picture frame comes crashing down onto the desk. The sounds of breaking glass, splintering wood, and cursing Tez can all be heard at once. "Oh no oh no oh no oh nooooo," he says.

"We better get out of here, like now," I whisper. I don't know why I'm whispering. The crashing sound was loud enough that I'm sure Chief Wolpaw heard it all the way in Fan du Lac. He'll probably be rolling up, sirens blazing, ready to take us to jail in a minute.

“Chrysler LeBaron,” Tez curses again, his voice shaking.

“I know,” I say. “We’re in huge trouble.”

“No,” he says. “Not that.” He holds his lantern close to the mangled frame. There, under the map that was displayed on the wall, is another map. My heart pounds faster and faster.

Tez carefully lifts off a shard of broken glass and peels back the outer map for a closer look. It’s the same landscape, for sure. The lake’s right in the middle, looking like it has horns and whatnot. Working the two maps apart, Tez all but falls back when he finally reveals the key at the bottom.

The title of this bottom map, ancient and yellowed and faded by time, is two words:

CAMP DEVILWOOD

19
Mr. Mystical

Tez

Corryn breaks the silence. "Who sends their kid to a place called *Camp Devilwood*?! Why not just go straight for Camp Murderface, am I right?"

I hear myself talking. "People live in Hell, Michigan. Weird names just become names after a while. Back home in Indiana, there's a town called Santa Claus."

"Yeah, well, in Pennsylvania, there's a town called Intercourse," Corryn informs me. "Even *they* think it's weird. There are T-shirts and postcards and everything."

Finally, my brain kicks back into gear. Specifically, the big gear marked TIME TO PANIC crashes into an equally big gear labeled SELF-PRESERVATION. Why are we just standing here talking about this?!

This is a bigger burglary job than I planned when I asked for bobby pins. We didn't just sneak in and invisibly steal some maps like master thieves. There's glass and wood and papers on the floor—everywhere! To be fair, there were already papers everywhere, but the glass and wood are new!

When Mrs. Winchelhauser gets here in the morning, it's going to be obvious: she got robbed. We're probably going to be arrested! And sent to jail! Where we might get shanked! Jeez-o-Pete, we're going to die. We're both going to die!

"We need to get out of here," I say.

Rolling up the two maps we found, I snatch a brochure for present-day Camp Sweetwater from the desk. That, I stuff into my pants, for real, and then grab my lantern. We got what we came for, and I'm getting out before we're done for.

"Tez, wait up," Corryn whispers urgently.

I didn't realize I was moving that fast. I just wanted to get away from the scene of our crime. I'm hot and itchy, and sweating everywhere. Everywhere. My chest hurts. Like, it really hurts; I have to stop before my heart gives up racing in exchange for a dirt nap.

Though I slow down, I keep moving. I feel like we're walking through a shadow world, a strange version of Camp Sweetwater that only exists at night. There are no lights—just my lantern and Corryn's.

They swing as we move, throwing flashes in every direction. I wonder—if someone looked out of a cabin right now, would they think we were the will-o'-the-wisp? We could become somebody's urban legend.

"Tez, stop!"

I do, mostly because Corryn's voice is loud. I'm sure she wakes the entire camp. Like, people in senior camp, all the way over on the other side of the lake, probably just sat up and want to know what's going on by the big, red Recreation Barn.

"Where are you even going?" Corryn demands.

"Away from the scene of the crime!" I don't say *obviously*. But obviously.

Corryn puts her lantern on the ground. Reaching out, she grabs my shoulders. She doesn't shake me, which is kind of a relief. "We're away. Take a breath, man. Jeez."

I put my lantern between my feet and do as she

says. My chest really hurts, my throat too. I'm kind of a precision instrument, and right now, I have too much humidity and adrenaline to function properly. Gulping at air, I nod to tell her I'm listening, but I don't really have the breath to talk yet.

"Everything's bonkers around here," she says sympathetically. "But it's going to be okay."

She's right. It is. We're going to make it okay. Sucking down another huge breath, I nod again. "The camp is messing with us."

"Exactly."

I must look really freaked out. And she doesn't even know half of the why. I *don't* want to get caught, for sure. But my chest won't stop hurting, and I'm afraid of what that means. It's a sharp, bright pain right in the middle of my chest. Every time my heart beats, the pain surges.

The lanterns cast backward shadows on our faces; we're drugstore horror covers in real life. Corryn is usually like, rub some dirt on it, buck up little camper (which is kind of hilarious, since we actually are campers).

But instead of giving me a noogie, she suddenly wraps her arms around me.

A hug. I haven't had a hug since my mom put me on

the camp bus. It wasn't even that long ago, but it feels like forever. It's warm and nice and makes me homesick. I miss home, where no one sleep-shaves their head, and nothing waits in the depths of a lake to drink my blood.

Corryn thumps my shoulder blade. "Hug me back, dummy."

So, I do. Finally, my pulse slows and the ache in my chest fades. For a minute, everything is all right again. The woods are deep and shaped around us, full of crickets and bird call. Frogs peep at the edge of the water, and even the sound of softly washing waves on the shore is comforting.

Corryn smells like sweat and geraniums, which makes sense. If she were a flower, she wouldn't be delicate or frilly. She'd be strong and tall, with unexpected brightness, just like geraniums. I probably shouldn't be noticing what she smells like. I'm not supposed to take any direct hits, and her boyfriend Elliot doesn't know that.

After a few seconds, I wriggle out of Corryn's embrace. In the dark, she can't see me blush. But I really do think it's more of a flush. Like a heat rash or something. It just goes everywhere, and that's embarrassing.

Clearing my throat, it takes me a couple of tries to say, "Thanks."

"I think at this point, it's basically my job to rescue you."

"I think it's our job to rescue each other," I reply, shuffling a little in place. "And this camp. And now that we have these maps, we can do just that."

June 11, 1983
Corryn

Somehow, Tez and I get back to our cabins and sleep—at least, I do.

Then we get through a whole normal day of camp, making flower crowns and playing jarts, and taking a nature hike where we were supposed to identify the trees. But Scary Mary and Gavin decided that we should just shut our gobs and *look* at the trees, so that's what we did.

After dinner, we sit in the Great Hall, the big room mostly empty and quiet after the raucous and ravenous herd that came and went. We linger, but not because we're enjoying extra helpings of dinner. I honestly don't even know what they served us tonight. It's some kind of mystery meat, and part of the mystery is whether or not it's even meat.

Tez and I study our notes. It's the first time we've had a chance since we've been back from the library. We have a bunch of scribbled details, and not all of them are exactly legible. Tez's handwriting is, if I'm being nice, a little . . . unconventional. To call it chicken scratch would be an insult to chickens.

It doesn't seem to slow Tez down at all, though. He's scanning the notes, speed-reading and muttering to himself. I've been doing the same but don't feel any closer to answers, and I'm further from sanity than when we started. Also, my eyes hurt.

I push back from the table and sigh. Tez doesn't even notice. He's focused. He is In the Zone.

"You must be one of those kids who gets an A in everything," I say.

"This is nothing like school though." He sweeps his arm across the table, scattering our notes. A scrap with a snippet of info about vampire devils lands on my tray and becomes soggy with meat goo. "School is easy. They give you the answers and you just study and spit them back. We don't know what the answers are here.

We don't even know the questions!"

He's right.

"Well, we have to start somewhere, and you said the best place to start would be where it started. That means Mechant's evil lodge or whatever."

"Yeah."

"Then what's the holdup here?"

Tez hums a little tune, then answers as if he's a TV game show host delivering the final clue. "Because we need the answer to the question, How do we get the campers home?"

Uhhhh. I say that in my head. Out loud, I say, "Well, that answer isn't going to be in these papers."

We sort through the notes again anyway, turning them over and back, flipping them into little piles like it's a game of Go Fish. Tez's handwriting really is horrible. "What does this one say?" I ask. "It looks like 'Be cool. French guys.'"

"Oh," Tez says with a snort. "That's just my to-do list."

I almost shoot some Mr. Hiss out of my nose. Mr. Hiss is a sort of off-brand Dr Pepper they serve here. I guess it would be too expensive to serve a drink that actually completed medical school.

"That very clearly says 'Mechant, French curse,'" Tez says, pointing to the paper.

"Sure," I say. "Sure it does. And what about this?" I slide him a paper with six words (or what looks like words) written on it.

"Those are the names of the girls who died," he says. He no longer sounds like a game show host. He sounds like he's reading a eulogy at a funeral. "Virginia Finch, Leigh Wade, Dorothy Duane."

I repeat the list after him. "Virginia Finch, Leigh Wade, Dorothy Duane . . . What, oh what, happened to you?"

"If only we could ask them," he says. "I thought about burning more devilwood. But one, I'm still traumatized from the last time. And two, more importantly, they don't seem to be able to say anything meaningful that way, you know?"

"Uh-huh," I say slowly. Where is he going with this?

His eyes widen. I can almost see the light bulb pop up above his head. "We could try scrying."

"What's that?" I ask.

Of course, Tez basically lives for people to say "lecture me on a subject," so total shock that he leaps right in, in a big way. He always waves his hands when he talks. Right now, it looks like he's trying to land fighter jets with the way he's throwing his limbs around.

"I'm not saying it will work, I mean, the Oracle of Delphi turned out—"

"To be a petro-stoner," I cut in. "The vapor, I got it, Mr. Mystical. Don't start at the beginning of time, Tez. Just explain what you want to do *now*."

"Let's find a smooth surface, and look into it, and try to call the ghosts forth." He lifts his chin. "It can be anything. A crystal ball—"

"Left mine in my other pants."

"Or a bowl of water, or—"

Now my light bulb goes off. "A mirror. Like Bloody Mary."

Tez blinks at me. "I'm not familiar."

This kid, seriously. He's killing me. Knows the Oracle of Delphi, clueless about Bloody Mary and how hapless kids like us call her forth from the great beyond. With a quick look around to locate our counselors, I grab Tez by the arm and almost drag him off his chair. I give him a look that says *let's go*, and he finally gets it in gear.

I lead him away from the Great Hall, up the path

that leads to the ball courts, and more important, a bathroom that nobody uses. It's too small, it always smells like goat butt, and there are definitely spiders in the latrine well.

When we get inside, I shudder. *Somebody's* been using it. Yikes.

Trying not to take a breath, I remind myself we're not going to be here long enough to worry about the stench. It's just a convenient place where we won't get interrupted.

But first, I have to set the stage. Bloody Mary needs a *dark* mirror. So that's what we're going to have. There's no door on the toilet stalls. That makes it easy to step up on a seat and unscrew the light bulb in the middle of the ceiling. Not all the way out. Just enough that darkness spills around us. It's not pitch-black; there's still moonlight coming in through the high ventilation windows.

"Uh, Corryn?"

I hop down, blinking at the dark. Flailing around, I accidentally whomp Tez in the head. But that helps me find his shoulder. Wrapping my hand around that, I say to him, "Okay, we have to look in the mirror. And instead of saying "Bloody Mary, 1-2-3," we're going to say their names. And when we do, they'll appear. Hopefully."

Skeptical, Tez says, "This doesn't sound very scientific."

My eyes adjust to the low light, and I bump/nudge Tez on purpose this time. Seriously, I've rolled my eyes more around him than I have around anyone in my entire life. And I currently live in a cabin with Ew. "Scrying was your idea, remember? Everybody knows about Bloody Mary—that means it works."

"What's supposed to happen? Can you ask questions?"

I start to give a snappy answer. How does he not know about this? Is he also unaware of the tale of the ghostly hitchhiker who disappears from your back seat, or the hook in the car door? Tez is both the smartest and the dumbest kid I know. One day, I'm gonna call and tell him it's coming from inside his house.

Just as I'm thinking that, I remember that if you tick Bloody Mary off, she's supposed to come through the mirror and kill you.

Oops.

Well, we've come too far now. Shouldering into Tez, I get us in place in front of the safety mirror and stare into it. The darkness makes us look eerie; I'm not even sure it's reflecting what's really behind us. Bad thought. Bad!

"Okay, let's do this," I say.

Then we say the names together. "Virginia Finch, Leigh Wade, Dorothy Duane. Virginia Finch, Leigh Wade, Dorothy Duane. Virginia Finch, Leigh Wade, Dorothy—"

Above us, the light bulb makes a funny pop. Then our two faces in the shiny metal mirror fade away to reveal the girls.

Whoa. Whoa-y whoa whoa. I really didn't expect this to work, but there they are. My neck prickles and I wrap my arms around myself.

There they are, clear as the yearbook, but with blood on their faces, and dirt in their hair. They look really, really young. And really, really scared. Virginia clutches her locket, and the other two huddle closer.

Beside me, Tez sucks in a sharp breath. So much for asking them questions. I hope he doesn't faint on me. I'm not sure how I'd explain that.

The girls in the mirror shift. Their eyes are dark. They beg. Their mouths move, but there's no sound. I'm really glad. I'm super glad there's no sound, because my idea or not, this is freaking me right out.

Help us, they mouth, and look behind themselves in terror. They turn back. Their mouths move in unison again. *In the pit. Help us.*

There's a roar. It rips right through us. Tez grabs me, clutching me, and I know we both hear it. Something awful. Something monstrous.

It roars, "Mine!"

The mirror goes black!

It explodes from the inside!

The metal bends toward us, like someone ran at it from behind and punched. Punched with a face that's narrow and demonic. An acrid, sulfurous stink bubbles up behind us, and all of a sudden, I hear a whole lot of flies buzzing.

That's enough for me.

I haul it out of the bathroom, Tez right on my heels. When we get into fresh air, he crashes into me. We barely stay on our feet. But as we peel apart, we don't have to say a word to each other. We know what this means. We were right. We have to help those girls get home.

And we just might die trying.

20
Blood Blood

Tez

Later, we sneak out to make a plan. It's both scarily possible and, for me, pretty easy to escape our cabins after curfew.

It's like Camp Sweetwater hired a couple of completely unqualified, possibly psychopathic teenagers to guard Oak Camp. I'm not saying that's what they *did*; I'm just saying that's what it's *like*. According to my mom, the simile guarantees it's not libel.

Anyway, Gavin will let anybody out of the cabin as long as we have a good metaphor for going to the bathroom. The lucky pass phrase tonight is "I've got to go make my bladder gladder."

Gavin finds this hysterical. This guarantees I'll never, ever say it again. However, it explains my funny walk as I escape from the cabin with several maps shoved into my tighty-whities.

It takes forever for Corryn to appear. When she finally does, she smells like the powder on my grandma's dresser had a slap fight with the perfume on my mom's. She's got glittery half-moons on each eyelid, not super visible because her brown eyes are narrowed. Also, her downturned lips are unnaturally pink. I mean, I've only got a lantern, and I can tell they're one shade off neon. I open my mouth, but she cuts me off.

"Don't say anything," she warns me, shaking her shower caddy at me. Then, before I can do it, she adds, "And that includes 'anything.'"

Did they hold her down and force her to get decorated? Was this her clever plan to escape? It's got to be the second. There's no way Ew was strong enough to hold Corryn down for craziness like this.

Ducking off the main path, I tell her, "Whatever sacrifice you made to the cause, I salute you."

With a grudging nod, Corryn mutters, "Okay, you can say that."

Deftly, we avoid the other cabins—but we also

stay in sight of the camp. Even though there are no wolves in Ohio, there are for sure: skunks, mosquitoes, snakes, possibly bears, and vampire devils (literal or metaphorical). Wandering aimlessly in the dark seems like a good way to end up sprayed, bitten, bitten, eaten, or possessed.

Corryn raises her lantern and points at the angular roof in the distance. "We can hide behind there."

The Arts and Crafts building, of course. It's tall and it sits at an angle to the rest of camp. We duck down behind it, nothing but forest to the back and camp to the front.

"Nobody can sneak up on us from here," Corryn says.

"Turn around," I reply.

She looks offended. "Why?"

I gesture at the paper tube running down the leg of my pajama pants. "Because."

Now Corryn's cheeks are supernatural salmon to go with her glitter lids and rosy lips. But she turns around, which I appreciate. Reaching into my pants, I pull out the maps. Then I make some slight readjustments; she doesn't need to see that either.

"Okay?" she asks.

I nod and drop to the ground with my lantern. "Okay."

The wall maps are still stuck together. Very carefully, I pick at the edge that reveals the camp's old name. Fortunately, they come apart quickly. Humidity and time must be the only things that glued them into one. I'm careful, because the one on the bottom is a lot more brittle. I pin that one down with my lantern, and the other down with Corryn's.

Dropping to the ground beside me, Corryn hums as she looks over the maps. Together, we study them for a long time in silence. Crickets chirp, taunting bats that flap away in trees. Above us, the clouds drift apart, revealing a perfect quarter moon.

After we both take in the maps, Corryn finally points at a path that leads past the band shell we have now. "That's where Primrose was. That's where they disappeared."

My shoulder rubs hers as I scan back and forth. "Okay, and up here is where we found the devilwood, I think."

"Definitely. We were up past the edge of the lake when we played Get Lost in the Woods."

I lift my lantern to get a better look. There are a lot of faint lines on the older map. It's hard to see them all in the dark. I trace my finger along the shore of the lake. Up past the east horn and into an area marked *Sweetwater Forest.* In the middle, right between the lake's horns, there's a little dotted line that makes a square.

With my nose pressed almost to the paper, I breathe in its old, acid scent. And I make out the words we've been searching for. I think.

"Right there," I say, pressing a finger into the paper. "It says Old Stone Wall. People don't just build walls in the middle of nowhere. Walls protect things. They keep things in, or . . . out."

"You wanna know what *I* think is weird?" Corryn asks, and doesn't wait for an answer. She gestures at the oldest map. "That thing says Camp Devilwood on it, but that name wasn't in any of the books. At least, I don't remember seeing it."

My questionable heart does a flip-flop. "Me either."

"That's something to put in your back pocket till later," she says. "How come this place has a secret devil-wood map, when nobody ever called it that?"

Spring peepers sing out in the woods, falling into

eerie time. There's the sound of the generator that runs the fridge in the Great Hall, a choir of frogs, and quiet. A long, uneasy quiet. "Definitely in the back pocket for later."

With a nod, Corryn goes back to the actual details of the map. She traces her finger along the path again, all the way back to the little square marked Old Stone Wall. "So, you think that's it? You think that's Mechant's lodge?"

"Yeah. Now we just need to get there."

"I can skip tennis tomorrow," Corryn says. Reaching down for her leg, she fakes a groan. "My knee still hurts."

"Your ankle," I remind her.

With a snort, she says, "My whatever. And you still haven't told me what you're doing instead of sports."

There's no way I'm telling her about my condition. She's my first real friend who treats me like a normal person. I'm not giving that up. But I do give her a cryptic smile. "Searching for three lost campers with you."

Rolling up the maps, Corryn informs me with absolute certainty, "One day, you're going to tell me."

I laugh. Maybe, one day, I will.

June 12, 1983

Corryn

I wake up buzzing with purpose and energy. Forget breakfast. Who needs Froot Loops and OJ when you're running on adrenaline?

I scamper up the path toward tennis and see Tez there, trying to look casual. He's leaning against a tree and whistling. His hair is unkempt, sticking up in spots like wild weeds. His eyes are ringed with bluish shadows. He shoots me an incredulous look.

"What?" I say.

"You're supposed to be limping," he grumbles. "Not gamboling."

"Hey, how do you know I play a mean game of—"

"Not gambling. GamBOLing!"

"What the heck is that?"

"It's what you were doing! It's like a cross between a skip and a jog. Now if Örn asks, show him this letter I prepared." Tez hands me a piece of official Camp Sweetwater stationery.

It's a letter addressed "To Whom It May Concern." The very neat handwriting indicates that I am to refrain from all sports-related activities due to a severe sprain of the left medial malleolus.

"Wow," I say, holding up the letter to the sun to examine its very impressive authenticity. "Is this what you do in your free time? Forge medical documents? Where did you get this letterhead? How did you write so neatly?"

"I went back to the office after you went to shower," he says. His eyes twinkle and he pulls the straightened bobby pins from his pocket.

"Without me?!" I say.

"You said you were going to die if you didn't scrub that goo off."

"Well, yeah! But that doesn't mean you get to go pull a B&E without me!"

"Sorry," he says. "What was I supposed to do, come by your cabin and throw gravel at the window?"

"Yeah!" I say. "Exactly that!"

"Okay, then I will next time," he says. "Now start limping or there won't be a next time."

I start my limp just as Örn comes running by on his way to the courts. He's got to be the absolute sweatiest person I've ever seen. He wears a headband, but it doesn't do a good job of keeping the sweat off his face or the hair out of his eyes. He looks like a shaggy dog caught in a rainstorm.

"Ready to roll, Corryn?" he asks me. "Hustle up. You only live once. Even if you do get to serve twice." He winks and offers up a sweaty hand for a high five. I guess this is what passes for tennis humor.

"Yeah, well, you know, my ankle is really bothering me again," I say. I add what I hope is a convincing wince.

"Martina Navratilova is gonna play the US Open with a bad back!" Örn says.

"Well, I'm not Martina Narva . . ."

"Björn Borg won Wimbledon on a busted knee!"

Tez interjects, "I'm sorry, what's a Björn Borg?"

"Björn Borg. Only the greatest Swede to hold a racket!" Örn says. Tez laughs. Örn is still holding his hand up for the high five.

I was raised right and know it's a sin to leave someone hanging, so I smack his palm with mine, even though I know I'll need to wash the Örn-sweat off later.

But as soon as my hand makes contact with Örn's meaty palm, his eyes go black. Both his eyes. Both his eyes are just suddenly all pupil. No iris, no, uh, whatever the white part is called. They're just two black pits, dull against the shiny gleam of his reddened, sweat-soaked face.

Tez and I look at each other in panic. The next words Örn says are not "Björn Borg" but rather "Blood *blood*." At least that what it sounds like he's saying. It sounds more like a gurgle in his throat than actual words. Also, his lips don't move. But he's definitely talking.

"Blood *blood*. Blood *blood*. Blood *blood*."

Forget the fake sprained ankle. Forget tennis. Forget everything!

I start to pull free, but all of a sudden, Örn twists my arm. He turns the high five into a stranglehold on my wrist. My fingers throb with my heartbeat.

"*We hunger*," Örn rasps. His voice is like the buzz of a chainsaw. His fingers are like claws, digging into my skin. "*We wait*."

Before I have time to scream, or to do anything really, Tez jumps between us. He's grabbing Örn's fingers and trying to pry them off me. His face is twisted into a scowl, and he grunts with exertion. But Örn is strong, his arms powerful with muscle.

For a second, I think about how weird we must look. Just me, Örn, and Tez holding hands outside the tennis courts. What would Scary Mary and Gavin say? But mostly I'm thinking about the pain. The searing, burning, cutting pain. It feels like Örn is going to rip my hand off. Like it might literally be removed from my wrist, leaving me with a bloody stump.

And then Örn lets go.

His slick hand slides off mine with an audible thwack. I look in his eyes and, besides a slight look of confusion, they are back to normal. They are brown and white in the right places. And a little wet. Örn might be the only person on earth with sweaty eyeballs.

"Edberg," he says.

Tez and I just stare at each other.

"Stefan Edberg," Örn continues. "They say he could be the next Björn Borg. We'll see. Hard to be better than Borg."

I can't stop clenching my wrist. There is a line of crimson half-moons from where Örn's fingernails dug into my flesh. It hurts like crazy. A tiny bubble of blood appears and then pops.

"What's wrong with your wrist?" Örn says. "I thought you hurt your ankle?"

"Ankle, wrist, foot, who knows what's what these days?" Tez says, grabbing me by the non-injured hand and pulling me away.

Örn shrugs. He turns back to his tennis-playing charges and sees that some of the campers have opened an equipment bag and are having some sort of a war with its contents.

"Hey!" Örn yells. "Those are my balls! Get your hands off my balls." He runs off after the cackling campers.

We flee in the opposite direction, sprained medial malleolus be darned.

Once we're far enough away from Örn to be out of earshot, Tez stops and stares at me. "Are you okay?" he asks. Then he immediately adds, "Sorry."

"What are you sorry for?" I ask. "You weren't the one who tried to rip my arm off. Örn was possessed!"

"I mean, I'm sorry for—" Tez cuts himself off. "Never mind."

"What?" I ask. He looks really upset. His face is an unnatural hue. He is literally biting his lip. Then he lets it all out.

"I mean, I'm sorry for asking if you're okay. I know how annoying that can be, you know?"

"I'm not sure I do know. I mean, it's actually kind of a nice switch to have somebody care about how I feel."

He goes on, "All people do at home is ask if I'm okay. My parents, my teachers, everyone. They're always, 'Oh, Tez are you okay?' Like I might break. Like I'm some delicate object. Like I'm a human Lycurgus Cup."

"Now you've kind of lost me." I guess his parents think he's a baby. Or a cup. Hey, mine think I'm an idiot. "I don't mind you asking. And the answer is yes, I totally am. At least I think I am." I rub my wrist again. It only hurts a little. "But Tez, whatever is happening here, it's getting worse."

Tez looks down at my arm with an expression that goes beyond concern. It's not fear; it's . . . I don't know what it is. It's weird.

"Should we just, like, forget this whole thing and run far away?" I ask. "Just start running and don't stop until we get home?"

"No," Tez says, and he startles me when he stomps his foot. It would probably be real dramatic if we weren't two kids hiding in the woods. Instead, it's kind of funny and I can't help but ask him, "Why not? Because you hate running?"

"No," he says. "Because I hate home."

I look hard at him. He's always saying "my mom" this, "my dad" that. Could his home really be that bad?

That he'd rather stay here and face . . . whatever this is? I know mine is, but . . .

It's like he's reading my mind because he says, "I'm serious, Corryn. I don't want to run and hide. I want to stay and fight. For you. For me. For camp."

When he says that, all kinds of weird, goony feelings stir around in my chest. What he's saying sounds like premium processed cheese, but it feels like truth. Like a cause. Like something bigger than us, and it's not even out of reach.

"For Camp Murderface," I say.

"For Camp Murderface," Tez agrees. Then he adds, "I'm not going to be afraid anymore. I'm not going to hide. I'm going to fight. I'm going to win."

"No, you're not," I say.

He looks hurt.

"*We* are," I say. "*We're* going to win."

Tez stops talking and turns to face me. He has a goober face and goober hair and I've mowed down dandelions that look stronger than him. But there's something about the certainty in his dark eyes that keeps me from making a smart-aleck remark. And for once he doesn't say anything eggheaded or bookish. He just raises his hand for a righteous high five.

"You're going to get my blood all over you," I say.

"And I," he says, as our hands smack together, the sound ringing out like a bolt of thunder. "Do. Not. Care."

Our joined hands stick together, like a promise. A swear.

A blood oath.

For Camp Murderface.

21
A Plan Half Baked

Tez

It's a lot harder to sneak away from camp in the daylight.

My forged note worked on Örn (pre- and postdevil versions), but there are a surprising number of grown-ups hanging around outside in good weather (along with approximately one hundred to one hundred fifty campers). It's probably less surprising that they all want to know where Corryn and I are going.

"I forgot my retainer and I have to get it. He's my forest buddy," Corryn tells one of the art counselors when she stops us on the path. Never mind that only the baby campers have to go places with buddies. Corryn really tries to sell it. For actually real, she breaks out puppy eyes.

Winnie, the art counselor, pushes back her beret and looks us over. I can practically feel her skepticism rays boring through my bones. It's a lower level of radiation, but it leaves me feeling kind of squirmy.

"Your buddy, mm-hmm." She looks to me, then back at Corryn. "Which camp are you in?"

Corryn grabs my arm and pulls me away, laughing heartily. And fakely. "I just remembered, I have my retainer in, ha ha HA!"

Heading back toward the tennis courts, Corryn says, "She was giving us the eye."

"She gave us two of them," I agree. "But at least they were brown and not portals to the pits of hell."

With a shudder, Corryn puts her hands on her hips and looks around. "Okay, we can't follow the paths."

"Nope," I say. "The fastest way to get where we're going is straight across the lake." According to the map, the Old Stone Wall is almost dead center between the lake's horns. I don't need to say that out loud; we both totally know. We look at the lake at the same time. The far shore looks misted over, and it shouldn't be. It's almost eighty degrees out.

"I bet nobody would notice if we stole one of the canoes and booked it."

Digging the toe of my sneaker into the gravel path, I squint at her. "I bet the evil monsters in the lake probably would."

"Oi!"

We both cringe. The voice is unmistakable. It's both scary and Mary in its volume. And it echoes on the water. And off the clouds. And across the entire country. It sails the ocean green in the year 1983, back to England.

Wherever she's from, there are people looking around saying, *Blimey! She's back!*

Scary Mary stalks over to us. "What are you little tosspots doing over here?!"

"Standing," Corryn says, entirely correctly.

"I can see that," Scary Mary growls back. She leans into our faces. The things they say about British teeth aren't universally true. Hers are very white, very straight, and scarily sharp. (Nobody ever said British teeth weren't sharp. Just to clarify. But Scary Mary's are especially sharp. Squaline, even. Which means shark-like.)

Poking a finger into my chest, Scary Mary says, "Correct me if I'm wrong, but Chickenlips is supposed to be helping the ickles with their finger painting, and you," she says, turning to Corryn, "are supposed to be playing tennis. Why ain't you neither?"

I don't know why it comes out of my mouth. It just does. "I forgot my retainer. She's going to help me find it."

The cackle that rolls out of Scary Mary sounds demonic. It's just her usual laugh, though. "Did she help you lose it, then? Rooted it right out with her tongue, did she?"

"Uh," I say.

"S'what I thought," Scary Mary crows.

I don't think she's smart enough to know semaphore or any other visual languages, but I have the feeling that the entire camp is going to know about this before dinner.

Then, just as fast as her laughter comes, it dies between her stupid squaline teeth. "Two beads from the both of you! Get your bums back where they belong!"

We hurry in the vague direction of the tennis courts—again. Corryn mutters under her breath, "What about the rest of our bodies?"

It makes me feel the slightest bit better that Corryn isn't 100 percent brave 100 percent of the time. Then again, my mom says there's a difference between brave and crazy, and maybe Corryn has figured that line out better than I have.

"Okay," I say once Scary Mary is out of sight. "We're going to sneak around the back of the band shell, up behind all the senior camp cabins, and go around."

"We're never going to get back before lunch."

"Probably not," I say. "But, upside: Gavin and Scary Mary will get in trouble for losing us."

Corryn gives me a tiny smile and a huge wink. We're on the move. We keep moving at a steady pace. Usually, if you act like you're supposed to be somewhere, people don't question it. Or so I've heard. Because everybody and their creepy old grandpa at Camp Sweetwater keeps questioning us.

Just as we get past the Great Hall, the possibly undead lifeguard steps in front of us.

"Turn around," he says. He fixes us in his watery stare, his desiccated, beef-jerky body between us and the band shell.

I have major respect for him. He doesn't ask us any stupid questions. It's pretty obvious he doesn't care why we're out of place. All that matters is that we are. (Perhaps the inter-living just have less time for shenanigans.)

Still, I say, "We're just trying—"

He cuts me off. "Get back to camp! The both of you! Before I take it on myself to bring back Old Squally!"

"Who's Old Squally?"

The Old Lifeguard's turkey neck wobbles as he smacks one sinewy hand into the other. "The camp paddle."

Corryn and I turn on our heels, and once again, we plod back toward the tennis courts. At this point, we're both super frustrated. Corryn's muttering gets even lower under her breath. I'm pretty sure she's mumbling words that would get her mouth washed out with soap. I wish she'd say them a little bit louder. I could use the education.

"This stinks!" she bleats finally. We stop at the fountain by the Great Hall and take turns gulping down mouthfuls of lukewarm water. It's not refreshing at all, but the day's getting hot. Nobody questions a couple of sweaty kids at a water fountain. (Hopefully.)

"We're just going to have to try when it's raining," I say. "Or at night."

Corryn glowers back where we left the Old Lifeguard. "Who does he even think he is? It's bad enough that he's a hundred years old. That old Merv was peeking into cabin windows the other day. Maybe somebody should threaten *him* with Old Squally."

Water burbles in my stomach. "Wait, what? You didn't tell me that."

Corryn crosses her arms over her chest. "Tez. Old buddy, old pal. We talk about vampire devils and how many wolves there are in Ohio."

"There aren't any . . . ohhh." I frown. "Corryn, seriously. We should tell somebody."

"Seriously," she says, like she's about to explain the universe to me. "They put Gavin and Scary Mary in charge of our safety. Do you think they care?"

Ugh. That's a good question. They actually make them sleep in our cabins with us. This would be great if they weren't sociopaths. Since they are, I have no choice but to question the hiring practices around here. Except, after my run-in with Mrs. Winchelhauser, and Corryn's run-in with Örn . . . I think I know why a couple of British serial killers are our counselors.

A little part of me wants to hope that everybody's awful here because they're being affected by the weirdness in camp—the bad thing. Maybe if we get rid of the vampire devils, this place will get super normal. Perhaps even super fun.

But for now, staring at the welts forming on Corryn's wrist, I hope we live long enough to get to fun.

I hope. I really, really hope.

June 13, 1983

Corryn

All day long, we're normal campers, Tez and me.

Specifically, we are campers who are *not* walking past each other between activities and making secret plans to go find other totally normal, extremely dead campers who totally want to go home.

After archery, I meet Tez by the water fountains. He has this thing about that being the least suspicious place to talk. Tez has a lot of weird ideas, to tell the truth. But it's not a bad call. The water fountains by the Great Hall are usually deserted.

"Okay," Tez says, pulling his shoulders back and lifting his chin. I think he is trying to look brave or something. "We're going to do this tonight."

"Like, tonight? Or like, night-night tonight?"

Tez deflates slightly. "What?"

I don't know how this kid can give a lecture on ancient board games, but he doesn't even understand plain English. "Right after dinner tonight? Or after lights-out tonight? Or the witching hour tonight?"

"I mean," Tez says, drifting into one of his random factoid modes. "Since ghosts are plainly real, and we're assuming vampire devils exist, then the witching hour might not be a bad idea. Traditionally, it's when the veil between the living and the dead thins and—"

Over the loudspeaker, a bell sounds. The camp director has a literal bell in the office and she rings it over the camp PA system to let us know when to change to our next activity.

Clapping Tez on the back, I say, "Meet me here next break; you can finish that sentence, okay?"

We split off in two different directions. I don't know why the girls in Oak Camp can't have archery the same time the boys in Oak Camp do, but that's just the way it is. I'm a pretty good shot, if you ask me. I can't do tricks or anything. But I bet I could ride to battle on Elliot and take out some enemies from bike-back. Bike-back is the same as horseback, basically.

When I meet Tez after the next bell, I share this opinion. He agrees with me, and says, "Bike-back Boudicca."

"Celtic lady who burned down London," I say,

before he can digress. What? I can know stuff. "This is the plan. We're going to sneak away after the bonfire. Gavin and Scary Mary always go off by themselves for a while then. That's our chance."

Caught short, Tez only nods.

"And we probably better stockpile gear now," I add. "I'm going to sneak a shovel out of the gardening shed."

"For what?"

"Because I like walking around in the dark with a shovel," I say sarcastically. "Come on, man! Because we're looking for dead bodies! They're probably buried!"

Getting into the spirit of things, Tez says, "Ooh! I'll go sneak some laundry bags."

It strikes me all of a sudden that we're really doing this. We're seriously going to go creeping in the night to find real people (*Virginia Finch*, *Leigh Wade*, *Dorothy Duane*, my brain chants) who really died.

We're going to dig them up and, I guess according to Tez, put their bones in laundry bags. And then what? Stow away in the camp shuttle and dump the bones in front of jolly Chief Wolpaw and his Push Broom Mustache?

I guess Tez reads my face, because he says, "We'll

just gather them up. And leave the bags and the shovel as a marker. That way, the police can come and do their jobs."

The bell rings before I can reply. We go our separate ways again. For an hour, I get down and dirty making egg-carton fire starters. This would be cool, except the only person who gets to start a fire is the counselor, and when we're done, we have to leave our cartons on a shelf.

This is annoying, so when I find Tez waiting at the water fountains with tiny braids in his hair, I kind of want to shove him. Not him, personally. He's just the only one there—with tiny, floss-filled plaits all over his head, in a rainbow of colors. He looks like a goon.

"Gag me," I say, reaching out to tug one of them. His hair is short, and the floss unravels at the slightest touch.

Not even embarrassed, Tez says, "The little kids from Bantam Camp put those in."

"The ankle biters?" I demand. "Why are you hanging out with them?"

Tez shrugs and doesn't answer. Instead, he says, "I stashed three laundry bags and a canteen in the dip under my cabin. You should put the shovel there too.

We're going to need flashlights instead of lanterns, I think. I can get those."

I guess we're moving forward, then. "The maps too. And something to mark them with."

"Good idea," Tez says, then looks up like he's mentally jotting a note. When he looks back at me, he says, "Can you think of anything else we need?"

"Holy water?" I joke.

"During crafts, I can make a cross out of sticks." Then thoughtfully he says, "And a Star of David. And an ankh. It's probably what you believe in, more than the shape."

I start to tell Tez I was just kidding. But at the last second, I don't. I kinda want to see what he comes up with. Plus, walking into the night with a half-baked plan, we need all the help we can get. And if that means asking Zoroaster or Zeus for intervention, so be it.

Nobody's called on them for centuries; they'll probably be glad to hear from us.

22
The Witching Hour

Corryn

Dad says "the witching hour" is really between three and four in the morning. I, however, check Ew's Swatch, and it reads a quarter till eleven.

I haven't been sleeping much. And with the night's errand in front of me, you'd think sleeping would be just about the furthest thing from my mind. It strikes me that this evening is both bone-chilling and bone-gathering.

Am I really doing this? Is a cross made out of yarn and popsicle sticks really going to protect us from a long-simmering ancient evil ready to burst out and claim fresh souls? What does a vampire devil even look like? The library book didn't have any illustrations, and my mind can't even begin to conjure up an image.

I'm sitting here in my bunk, listening to the rhythmic breath of my cabinmates and the soft sounds of night. I have to remind myself that the vampire devils could still be metaphorical, and after all, we're not searching for *them*. We're searching for the girls. So really, it's just a bit of light grave robbery.

The ghosts—no, the girls—their names play like a tape on an endless loop in my mind. *Virginia Finch*, *Leigh Wade*, *Dorothy Duane*. They become a melody, echoing like a lullaby in my head. *Virginia Finch*, *Leigh Wade*, *Doro* . . .

Suddenly, I'm startled by a sound like fingernails tapping impatiently on a wooden desk. What's that? What's happening? Who's there? What's going on? Who am I? Why are things?

I am out of bed and standing in the middle of the room in half a second. I must have fallen asleep. Impossible! I hear the tapping noise again. It's coming from the window. Tez! He is here for me, throwing pebbles at the window to wake me up! It's time!

I rush out to meet him in the darkness. I close the door carefully behind me so as not to awaken Scary

Mary. Then we'd have problems bigger than ghosts to deal with.

Tez stands there with his flashlight pointed up under his chin, giving his face a wicked glow. "Took you long enough," he says.

"Shut up."

"Were you sleeping? I couldn't sleep."

"Shut up."

"Where's your shovel?"

"Shut up." Exhaustion has reduced my vocabulary to two words apparently.

"I'm serious," he says. "You said you were going to snag a shovel from the gardening shed."

"Well," I say. "I forgot."

"It's fine," he says. "I'm prepared. I have an extra."

"Ye of little faith," I say. "I can't believe you thought I'd forget!"

Tez rolls his eyes at me and then switches off the flashlight. "Come on," he whispers.

I'm starting to wake up and rally to the cause. "Why'd you turn off the light?" I ask.

"I've got this down," he says.

"You have the whole camp memorized in darkness?"

"Pretty much. I studied it all day."

Of course, I believe him. So we walk.

The stars are too far away to help us and the moon doesn't seem to care. We make our way toward the lake beneath the unlit sky. Just one foot in front of the other, moving in darkness, almost like a dream. Every so often, I ask Tez the capital of a particular state, to make sure we're not getting separated.

The farther we get from our cabins—and the closer we get to the lake—the darker it gets. There are fewer stray lights illuminating patches of ground. It grows darker and darker and darker still.

Suddenly, a howl pierces the quiet! I jump. A moment of quiet and then, *ahoooooo*, another howl. I clap a hand down on some part of Tez (maybe a shoulder?) and yank him hard to a stop. Cold fear sizzles through me.

"Relax," Tez says. "There are no wolves in Ohio."

"No doy! That's why the howling is a BAD THING!"

And what's worse is that it is getting closer.

Tez

The underbrush rustles.

Something mad and wild crashes through it. There

are more howls too. There *aren't* wolves in Ohio. But something *is* closing on us.

Blood pounds in my ears. My skin prickles everywhere. Evolutionarily, that was probably pretty handy once. It probably, long ago, made all of my fur stand up. It made me look bigger, so that predators would think twice about eating me. But that was *australopithecus* Tez, and I'm Tez *sapiens*. I don't have fur, but I do have a brain.

"Back up," I say as I catch hold of Corryn's shoulder. I pull her back against a huge oak tree. Gnarls dig into my spine, but the branches spread wide above us. This is a sheltering tree, and it feels safe. Solid. And climbable, if we need to escape upward.

Corryn's breath whistles a little. "If there are werewolves *and* vampire devils, I'm officially in over my head. As you would say, divorce schmivorce. I'll break my ankle in front of Örn on purpose if I have to."

I wish I could say that there are no *were*wolves in Ohio, but I don't know. It seems unlikely. The amount of cellular energy it would take to transform a human being into a wolf would basically fuel an entire nuclear power plant. And that kind of incredible cellular growth and transformation seems more likely to turn somebody into a weretumor than anything else.

But then again, ghosts shouldn't happen either and vampire devils are looking more likely every day. I know a lot of stuff, but maybe everybody back home is right: I don't really know everything.

Another crash. Another howl.

The sound shatters my thoughts. Turning, I can barely make out Corryn's face in the dark. Eyes squeezed closed, she looks like she's gritting her teeth.

Briefly, I wonder if I should hug her. That's how she calmed me down when I was freaking out. But I have this feeling that if I did, she'd punch me in the shoulder and call me a doofus.

That's not something I would take personally coming from her, but it seems like the wrong choice for the situation.

AHOOOOOOOO!

The howl is so close this time, I can tell it's coming from the east. Consulting my mental map, that's the direction of the Old Stone Wall . . . but there's something else just on the other side of that as well. Right around the east horn of the lake.

We're trying to be stealthy, but our midnight howler isn't—at all. Reaching into my backpack, I pull out a flashlight. The beast crashes toward us. I raise the flashlight. But I don't strike. I flick it on.

"Tastes great," howls a gangly, pimply kid wearing a Camp Sweetwater T-shirt. "Less filling!"

Then he pulls off his shirt. Waving it around his head like a lasso, he charges away. He leaves the waft of beer behind. It's bitter and skunky, but nicely familiar too. It's like Sunday afternoons when my uncles come over to watch the game with my mom.

Beside me, Corryn melts with relief. "It's just some dingus from senior camp," she says, exhaling.

"I think it might be a *counselor* from senior camp," I add.

Feeling warm and loose, I turn off the flashlight. Rubbing my chest, I urge my heart to settle down. My breath slows with it. When I finally open my eyes, the world seems clearer. The dark isn't as ominous.

Its mystery is stripped away now. No matter what monsters we might be facing, some things around here are just regular summer camp weirdness.

The kids walking around with mouths stained red have just been drinking bug juice, farts into a fan are high comedy, and we're creating crafts by the metric ton every single day, but the shelves never seem to fill up. And, sometimes, kids from the senior camp paint stripes down their noses with zinc oxide and run madly through the woods.

"All right," Corryn says, pushing off the tree. Her voice is back to normal. "Which way, map brain?"

"Hold on to my backpack," I say. "We're almost there."

Her mouth drops open in . . . shock? Offense? "I'm not holding on to your backpack. This isn't kindergarten!"

With a shrug, I say, "Suit yourself," and then start back in the direction of the Old Stone Wall.

The woods catch up in a hush. A mourning dove moans in the canopy above us; crickets reply with anxious chirps. In the distance, off my right hand, the tiny spring peepers sing along the shore. Corryn has iron in her beak. I have an encyclopedia of pathfinding crammed in my head.

When the soft thump of canoes tied up in the boathouse subsides, I know we're exactly halfway between the lake's horns. Now is the tricky part—looking for something that might not be standing anymore. I tuck my flashlight under my T-shirt, and turn it on.

The fabric dims the light. It shouldn't draw anyone's attention, but it's enough for us to start searching the ground.

"I don't see a wall," Corryn says. "But there's a ditch over here."

Walking carefully, I lean over, staring at the ground. Corryn's right—there's a dip in the ground, and it runs in a straight line. That means it's man-made. In general, if basalt isn't involved, nature doesn't make straight lines.

"This could be the foundation of the lodge."

"Or it could just be a ditch."

She's not arguing with me. She sounds thoughtful. Either way, an unnatural feature right where the map marks out the Old Stone Wall is definitely a find. We should mark it for sure, and then investigate more carefully. I have paper flags that I perhaps, maybe, have liberated from the supply closet.

I let my backpack slide off, then nearly strangle myself on the strap from my canteen. Freeing myself, I put my hands on my hips and glance around. "Okay. Let's see what we're working with."

Corryn nods. She drops her backpack too.

And then the ground swallows us whole.

23
The Bone Zone

Corryn

My first thought is that I still must be sleeping.

This feels exactly like a dream. Exactly like a *nightmare*. One second, we're standing in the woods, surveying the scene—or what we can make out in the muted glow of our flashlights—and then the ground gives way.

It's like when you go to sit down and some toad-licker pulls your chair out from under you. Only times a million. I can't help it. *Alice in Wonderland*—the book, not the girl—tumbles through my head: *Either this hole is very deep or we are falling very slowly.* I feel my stomach tilt-a-whirling and my arms flying uncontrollably above my head. I'm grasping and reaching, but my hands find only air.

"Tez!" I yell, and when I don't hear a response my blood turns to ice.

I stop falling, though my feet are hardly on solid ground. I feel like I'm in the ball pit at Funworld. Things roll under my feet, and a musty smell assaults my nose. I don't know what it is. My lizard brain screams, though—*this is bad.*

I yowl Tez's name again. This dark, awful place swallows up my voice. It doesn't even echo. It just disappears. When I cry out for Tez, the only answer is silence.

He's dead, I think in a panic. That's when I lose my balance. I trip right over, crashing into the ground. Not the ground. Into shapes—cool, rattling, *bad* shapes. I scream and scream and then, when a cold hand lands on my arm, I scream again.

I turn to see the source of the hand. I start to punch it because it's probably undead. When I realize it's Tez, I go ahead and punch him in the face out of stupid, angry relief.

“What the—?” he says. He doesn’t sound mad, although his brown eyes do look a little wounded. He rubs his chin and waits for me to explain.

“I thought you were dead!” I say. “I screamed your name and you didn’t respond!”

“I was a little distracted,” he says.

“Well, me too!”

“By the bones.”

“Right! The—what?!”

Tez points his flashlight around this—what is this? A cave? A cavern? A pit? The beam from the flashlight follows the smooth line of the wall, and as my eyes adjust, I start to feel claustrophobic.

It’s about the size of our cellar at home, and I never feel quite right down there. I feel like I can’t breathe. Like I’m in a coffin. Is that what this room is—a cellar? Whatever it is, Tez is right. It is *full* of bones. We are up to our waists in dozens—hundreds? thousands?—of dry, hard, clattering, chattering bones. I feel like I’m going to be sick.

“How do we get out of here?” I ask. The words feel like I’m barfing them.

“Good question,” he says. “But not the most pressing one.”

"Oh really, Tez? The most pressing question is *not* how do we get out of this giant pit of bones? Please don't make me punch you in the face again."

"The most pressing question," he says, "is *why* is there a pit of bones in the first place? I mean, sure, there are some bone-collecting predators who end up amassing impressive collections of carcasses, but I sort of doubt that there are hyenas here . . ."

"Really?" I say, my voice taking on what I realize is a nasty tone of hostile mockery. "You think this is the work of bone-collecting predators? You think this is a time for a lecture on the feeding habits of carnivorous mammals? Really oh really? You think that these bones are all from deer and one of them just happened to have the rather unusual deer habit of wearing a deer necklace of camp beads from deer camp around her deer neck?"

I pick up a string of Camp Sweetwater beads from the stack of bones next to me and fling them at Tez. He ducks, and the beads hit the bone pile and rattle eerily.

Tez's eyes get wide. "Whoa! Where were those?!" he asks.

"Right here." I point to my left where I found the beads.

He sweeps his flashlight around. Bright spots of

colors show up between gray. The beam finds a purple bead. Then a blue one, then a yellow. Bead after bead after bead strung through the stacks of bones.

And now that I'm not overcome with panic, I see more than beads. I see ribs. I see arms. I see skulls. *Human* skulls.

"It's time to face facts, Tez. The two-hearted vampire devils? Are definitely *not* a metaphor."

Tez

Bones are dead things. They can't hurt me. They can't hurt Corryn.

This is what I tell myself, but it's hard to believe. I don't have to be a paleontologist to know these bones aren't ancient burials. Honestly, even Gavin and Scary Mary would be able to figure that out.

Ancient remains don't wear plastic beads, and they don't wear button-up boots. Or ivory hair combs. Or lacy dresses. Scraps of clothing hold some of the skeletons together.

There are other glimpses of life too. A pocket watch glints dully in the corner. There's a rotting hatchet down here too. And worst of all, the air smells like decay. Rusty and tangy, pressing in from all sides.

I turn the flashlight overhead. The surface seems impossibly far away. But even though I'm sick down to my (*bonesbonesbones*) guts, even though my heart is starting to pound against my chest, I have to keep it together.

Corryn's been brave this whole time. But she gave me a right hook to the jaw a second ago, and she threw those beads pretty hard. She's falling apart.

And then a thought I had earlier comes back again. I felt brave in town, but scared in camp. Corryn's brave on the other side of the lake, but not on this one. And every single grown-up around us is terrible. Could it be this place? Could the evil that lives here be seeping into all of them—into her?

No. I won't even think it.

All I can do is try to look at this as logically as possible. I'm pretty sure if I don't, we're both going to die.

"We can climb up," I tell Corryn, though I'm not sure we can.

I take a step toward her and shudder. It feels like fleshless hands try to grasp my ankles. When I move, pieces of skeleton roll and shift around me. Though I don't want to notice it, I do. All around us, jaws hang from the skulls, wide open, screaming silently forever.

Still caustic, Corryn demands, "How? Did you learn how to make a bone ladder in one of your books?"

"No," I tell her, "I'm going to boost you up. And then you're going to go back to camp and get help."

When Corryn laughs, it's this terrible, high-pitched sound. It's not normal; it's not *her*. Except, it is her—out of her mind with fear. "Hey, genius, I followed *you* here, remember?"

"You have iron in your beak," I say. Hot tears sting my eyes. I have to pretend to be calm, but I'm not. I'm afraid. And my best friend at camp—maybe my best friend ever—is losing it. I force myself to wade closer to her. I won't look down. I can't look down.

When I reach her, I put my hands on her shoulders. "Hey. Hey. Corryn. We did it. Concentrate on that. We said we were going to find them, and we did. Now you just have to get back to camp and get help. We save each other, remember?"

For a moment, Corryn is silent. Then, slowly, she nods. "I remember."

"We're going to get them home," I tell her. "We're going to get *us* home."

All of a sudden, my flashlight dims. Bones around us shift. They settle, rattling like dice. I clutch Corryn's shoulders a little tighter. Inside my chest, my heart feels like a bag of Jell-O, squashed mercilessly by an angry fist.

The moment my flashlight goes dark, little sparks of light flicker up. They're orange and red and gold . . . they look like embers.

More of these embers drift up. They swirl around us, pulsing brighter, until the bone pit is exposed by a fierce, fire-like glow. We really are surrounded by bodies. This isn't some cave; it's perfectly square.

It's a room.

In a distant, dark corner, there are a few rotted beams jutting up, and one wall is lined with stones. Looks like we found Mechant's lodge after all.

"Tez," Corryn murmurs, and I drag my gaze to her face.

The unearthly fire has warmed her skin. Her hair floats up on currents of heat. Her dark eyes are turned toward something, and I follow her gaze. A swirling ball of flame hovers above three skeletons, smaller than the rest. The fire sinks; it's strangely alive. Then it splits into three fiery tails trailing down to each skull.

At once, shapes rise to the flames' surface. Not shapes. Faces. People.

Virginia Finch. Leigh Wade. Dorothy Duane.

24
Helppleasehelp

Tez

The fire goes on—no source, no kindling, no nothing.

The girls in the flames shimmer and float, and for once, they're not screaming. They just look sad. Echoes of the past waver around us. It seems like there should be heat too, but the air is still wet and cool. It still makes my bones ache.

A sound rises, and I freeze. Corryn does too. I can barely hear her breathing.

It's like the fire in Primrose Camp all over. Only this time, we are hearing them as well as seeing them. We hear three girls making friends on the first day of camp. Their ghostly voices giggle and laugh; they sing an old-fashioned song in sweet little voices. They whisper secrets, they promise to be friends forever.

And then they change. I hear myself in Virginia's voice, the same anxiety and panic I felt after Corryn and I broke into the camp director's office. And in Dorothy's voice, I hear cutting sarcasm that reminds me of Corryn on this very night. The camp wanted them to be afraid too.

I hear it in those ghostly voices from the past, the fear even as they try to reassure each other. The darkness, even as they decide to become blood sisters.

I see them in the fire as real as if they are in front of me. Dorothy, Leigh, Virginia. They sit in a circle in the tent, their legs crossed, their knees touching in the small space. I see piles of beads on the ground, scattered like fallen leaves. They must have been really proud to win those beads. All for what?

The three girls stare straight ahead and take each other's hands. Virginia speaks first. "Sisters forever?" she says, her voice shaky.

"Sisters forever," Dorothy says.

"Sisters forever," Leigh says. Her voice is the shakiest of the three. It sounds like she might cry.

And then, just like the clippers in my cabin, Leigh's

pocketknife rises up and draws first blood. We hear it *schick* through the air. It sounds wet and slow, cutting into flesh.

Just like something took over Bowl Cut and Ew and Örn, controlling them like puppets, that *thing* drove Dorothy, Leigh, and Virginia into the woods. Around the horns of the lake.

Into the Mechants' cellar.

Their voices rattle the bones around us. Struggling against the force that holds us, Corryn whimpers.

"Ours," something says.

The sound comes from everywhere at once. It pricks sharp fear into my skin; this voice doesn't belong to Virginia or Dorothy or Leigh. The one that fell from Örn's lips when his eyes went black.

These girls say they want to go home.

"This is home now," the other voice replies. I feel it echoing in my bones. It's like it's inside the marrow, making itself part of my DNA. "Forever. Forever!"

A small explosion rocks one end of the cellar. Sharp white shards of bone fly. Corryn and I collapse to the floor, and she slumps against me. The fire fades; the voices, the ghosts, are gone.

When the last ember falls, my flashlight beams

back to life. Its cold, clear light falls on one of the girls' skeletons. A small, golden locket lies among the remains. Virginia's locket.

"Wait here," I tell Corryn. I crunch over and pick it up. That will be proof that we found them, found our missing campcestors here in this pit of bones. Stuffing it into my pocket, I start to walk back. Then I realize—a locket alone, the beads alone, probably aren't enough to make people believe our story.

Unscrewing the cap of my canteen, I dip down. For a moment, I hesitate. These aren't like bones in a museum, thousands of years old. I know the faces that go with these skulls. They're people. It feels wrong to disturb them. But we can't get them home unless I do.

I whisper, "Sorry," and then pick up bones that can't be mistaken for an animal's: the two that make up Dorothy Duane's opposable thumb. Dropping them in the canteen so they can't possibly get lost, I twist the cap closed above them. When they sink to the bottom, they make a soft *tunk*.

"Time to get out—" I say.

A terrible rumbling cuts me off. It sounds like bones grinding together. It sounds like a hail of teeth and ribs. It sounds like death, a shrieking groan that cuts through us. I take a step toward Corryn and my foot sinks down. Then the other does.

The cellar lurches, almost like it's coming alive.

"Tez?" Corryn says. The panic hasn't hit her again. Not quite yet.

Another step, and I sink deeper. There's something beneath the bones. Something that feels liquid—like quicksand. The dark voice rises again.

"No! You can't take them. You won't take them! You're our prize now!"

Corryn throws out her arms. She's trying to keep her balance, but she's sinking too.

"Corryn!"

"Tez!"

We both struggle toward each other. The pit swallows us even faster. It's like we're being crushed down a fleshy gullet, swallowed whole. Bones rise to our armpits now. They chuck and clatter. Skulls chatter, their teeth clacking together. They mock us as we're swallowed up.

Corryn reaches for me. "Grab my hand!"

I try. I'm not sure what good it will do. But then my fingers brush against hers, and we get swept apart.

Summer camp was supposed to be fun. It was

supposed to be amazing. It was supposed to be adventures and wonders and new friends and exciting new memories.

Then I realized, it had been. Even if it was only for a few days, I got all of that. Because of Corryn. I shout over the unearthly collapse of the cellar, "You're my best friend, Corryn. You know that, right?!"

"You're my best friend too," she shouts back. She sounds like she might be crying. "Elliot's second best. I mean that!"

As I'm dragged down further, the bones wash over my shoulders. But I still feel a brief flare of warmth. Of happiness. "You're the coolest person I know," I choke.

"You're not cool at all," Corryn sniffles. "But you're awesome."

Bones rise above my chin. I shudder, trying to talk to her without opening my mouth. Maybe I have to die tonight. But I don't have to choke to death on evil bones. "If we turn into ghosts, I'll try to find you!"

Corryn doesn't answer. Or if she does, I can't hear her.

With one last, horrendous tug, I'm dragged into the dark.

Corryn

As the tide of bones drags me down to death, my outstretched hand finds Tez's.

We're going down, down, down. *We never took that bike back. I made him steal it.* Tez clasps my hand. *Who cares when we're together?* I close my eyes and wonder if you can drown in bones.

I think of Dad, of Mom, of Elliot, of all I've left. All the time I spent being mad at my parents. Wasted time. I don't know why they lied to me about the divorce, but I know they made sure they both told me they loved me before I left for camp.

Screams and howls and roars torture my ears and threaten to explode my skull. They get inside my brain, and I think these are the last sounds I'm going to hear. A wailing cry melting me from the inside, ushering me off this plane.

I feel something like fingers dragging across my skin and an invisible force pulling at my hair. It feels like the thing in the lake, only it's never going to stop pulling. Down, down, down. The terrible voices crackle in my skull, the unholy reality of this living nightmare staring me in the face.

And then I get clocked in the head. I see sparkly

little stars inside my brain and hear a voice screaming, "Hold on!"

Hold on? Holding on is all I'm trying to do.

"To the ring!" the voice says.

The ring? What ring? The voice is gruff but warm and somewhat familiar. Then I realize, the heavy thing above me isn't a bone. It's a life ring from the boat house.

I grab it with one hand and grip Tez with my other. The ring is large, like two feet across. It has ropes on it that dig into my wrist as I get pulled up from the pit of bones. Something down there is still tugging, still dragging, still sucking us underneath with invisible force.

"Dead man's float!" the voice yells. I've definitely heard that voice before. It's too dark to see anything, but . . . could it be? I squeeze the rope and the ring like I'm gripping Elliot's handlebars on the wildest ride of my life. I squeeze Tez's hand even harder.

Slowly, slowly, inch by inch. It feels like a game of tug-of-war we're just barely losing, but we're winning. Because we're getting out of here. We're getting out of here! Me and Tez, getting dragged like it's red rover, red rover, and we're finally coming over.

We're up on solid ground. We're surrounded by air, not bones. We can breathe! Our unseen rescuer turns the beam of his flashlight on himself. It lights him up like a star on Broadway. I recognize him immediately.

It's the Old Lifeguard! The creeper. The paddle threatener. The one who should have been dead a long, long time ago.

I throw down the life ring and jump into his arms. I squeeze him in the world's strongest hug.

"Settle down, girl," he says. "You're safe. Stop your struggling!"

"How did you find us?" Tez asks, barely able to catch his breath.

The Old Lifeguard sighs a long, slow sigh. His exhalation makes his mustache hairs flutter like daisies in a gentle breeze. "I don't know if you noticed, son, but I'm a lifeguard. It's my job to guard your lives."

A little edge to his voice, Tez asks, "Is it your job to peek into our cabins?"

"I check on *all* the cabins," the Old Lifeguard says. "After everybody's supposed to be asleep."

"Why?" Tez asks.

The Old Lifeguard doesn't answer. He just looks toward the pit and, as if addressing someone—or something—there, says in a low, slow voice, "They never learn."

“Who never learns? Never learns what?”

Again, no answer. Just a grunt and a nod and a gruff “Let’s get out of here before it’s too late.”

He flicks the beam of his flashlight toward the path ahead. I turn to look back at the pit of bones, but without the illumination of the flashlight, all I see is darkness. We fall in line behind the Old Lifeguard and make our way out of the Mechants’ lodge.

Behind us, awful, evil laughter echoes on.

25
The Shortcut

June 14, 1983

Tez

I still can't believe we're alive.

I still can't believe that a lifeguard who has to be at least a hundred years old just fished us out of a supernatural pit of bones. I can't believe the witching hour has barely started and we're not even done, which means I'd probably better stop marveling over this stuff and get back to it.

Marveling sounds like a happy word anyway. Full of admiration or something, instead of just startled by the strangeness of it.

"Which way are we going?" I ask, trying not to look

back at the gaping pit in the forest. Also, I'm trying not to look at the darkened forest. I was approximately nine thousand times braver and/or stupider walking out here in the dark than I am right now. We almost *died*. It's my fault that Corryn almost died.

The Old Lifeguard says, "We're taking a shortcut."

"There isn't one," I say. I don't *want* to contradict him, but facts are facts.

"Let me tell you kids something. There's always a shortcut."

Corryn stays close to the Old Lifeguard. The circle of light cast by his flashlight is small and dim, but it's *something*. He's a grown-up. He wears an official Camp Staff polo shirt and a whistle around his neck. He makes it not dark. It's almost exactly the same thing as being safe.

I feel more wary, because *there's always a shortcut* sounds like it could be a line from a movie. In fact, I think it is. I start racking my brain, trying to remember which one. But when I let myself think, I see bones. Skeletal hands. Snapping teeth. Empty eye sockets. For once in my life, I think I'm going to stop thinking and just move.

At least, until I realize which way the Old Lifeguard

is leading us. It's those real-world wayfinding skills—the spring peepers get louder. The air tastes more and more like wet stone. A chill creeps out, and not a supernatural one, either.

"Why are you taking us to the lake?" I demand.

"Boy," the Old Lifeguard says, annoyed.

"We're too tired to swim across," I point out. "And I one hundred percent guarantee that we can't walk on water."

With another frown, the Old Lifeguard says, "You really are a pain in my caboose. Are you coming or not?"

I stop, staring at him. Mist crawls through the underbrush. Pale and strange, it wavers, swirling around our ankles and rippling against tree trunks. The veil is still thin. Our ghosts still aren't safely home. I finally understand what dread is: a mixture of fear and certainty.

Clearing my throat, I say, "I don't think we should trust him, Corryn."

Corryn stares at me like I started wearing underpants on my head. "He just saved our lives."

"Or maybe he wants us to *think* he did," I say.

Now Corryn hesitates. We've been through a lot together. It feels good that she hesitates and considers what I'm saying. Glancing back at the Old Lifeguard, Corryn wraps her arms around herself. Then she lifts her chin and asks, "So how did you know what we were doing anyway?"

Pointing the flashlight at me, then at her, the Old Lifeguard says, "Because I've been trying to stop you from doing it since you got here!"

"But *we* didn't even know what we were doing until a couple of days ago," I say.

Corryn nods. "And we didn't decide until today that tonight was the night."

It really, really looks like the Old Lifeguard wants to paddle us both. Like, he might sit down and carve a whole new paddle and christen it in our honor. But instead of that, which would take a lot of effort, he rolls his eyes. Then he drops the flashlight by his side and steps toward me.

With a lunge, Corryn grabs his arm. "Don't hit him!"

"Simmer down," the Old Lifeguard snaps. And then he shakes her off and . . . walks past me. He steps out of the tree line and onto the shore. We were even closer to the lake than I realized. As Corryn slips in next to me, we watch as the Old Lifeguard sets down the flashlight and . . .

Turns over a canoe. He looks back at us one more time, and says, "I'm not begging you. You can walk for all I care."

My face gets hot. He hadn't been wrong. There is always a shortcut. Directly across the lake.

Licking my dry lips, I finally whisper, "It does seem kind of stupid to row across a lake to save us from certain death just to row us back out to the lake and into certain death."

"If he does anything weird," Corryn promises me, "I'll deck him with an oar."

We nod at each other at the same time. It doesn't take long for us to climb into the canoe. Soon, the Old Lifeguard has us gliding across the water. His flashlight sits on the prow, leading the way with a long, silvery beam. Anyone could look out to the lake and see us. Knowing that makes me feel safer.

And since we're safer, since the cellar recedes with every stroke of the paddle, I feel braver. Clutching the strap of my canteen, I find my voice. "Can I ask you something?"

"Besides that?" the Old Lifeguard *and* Corryn say at the same time. She grins and elbows me gently in the ribs.

My fault for walking into it. But I lean against Corryn anyway. I know I can count on her to be real. She trusted me with her life—I'm going to do my best to be more careful with it from here on out.

"Yes, besides that. How did you know where we were going?"

"Because that's where they always go," the Old Lifeguard replies.

"They?" Corryn sounds dangerously skeptical.

The Old Lifeguard looks back at us. "People have a way of disappearing around Lake Sweetwater. And no matter how hard I try to stop it, well . . . they've been disappearing around here for a long time."

The way he says that makes me shudder. Corryn presses her shoulder against mine. "We read about it. In a book at the library."

"Did you?" the Old Lifeguard says noncommittally. Water laps around the boat, kissed by the oars, waving away toward the shores in a steady rhythm. It's almost peaceful. Almost enough to distract us from the conversation. But only almost.

I nod. "Yeah. One about the battle for Fan du Lac's soul."

“Mmm,” the Old Lifeguard says. “Crazy Amelie Beauregard’s book. She paid an awful lot to print those up. Gave them to the whole town. She was worse with those things than Boyd Gardner is when his zucchinis come in.”

“It was in the library,” Corryn says.

“I expect it was,” the Old Lifeguard says. He looks back, amused. “She built the library.”

The edges of this conversation seem to be slipping out of control. I would ask him just how old he is, but I think we already know. Instead, I challenge him from the side. “You’re saying it’s all a bunch of baloney.”

A jolt runs through us, a terrible crunching sound rushing up beneath the canoe. Before we can even cry out, the Old Lifeguard jumps from the boat and grabs the rope on the bow. He hauls the whole thing onto dry land . . . right next to the dock where Nostrils kicked me in the face and Corryn took her terrifying swim test.

The Old Lifeguard offers Corryn a hand, helping her out of the boat. Then he turns back to offer me one too. Before he grabs his flashlight, he looms in front of both of us. The shadows seem to climb into the cavernous wrinkles on his face. His mustache casts its own shadow, even. He really does look ancient.

"I never said such a thing," the Old Lifeguard says. "And I never would."

"Why not?" Corryn demands.

With a sweep of his hand, the Old Lifeguard claims the flashlight and starts walking toward the camp.

"Because my mama taught me not to lie."

Corryn grabs my arm and we run after him. "Where are you going?! We have to tell somebody we found them. We have to wake up the director! We have to call the police!"

"You go right on ahead," he says. "It won't make a lick of difference. Never has. Never will."

He has to be wrong. We found them. Dorothy, Virginia, Leigh. We found their bones. We found their resting place. And more than that, we have proof.

They *have* to listen to us.

Corryn

My sea legs are a little wobbly from the boat, and I kind of feel like I'm falling forward more than walking.

I'm definitely walking, though. As fast as I can,

without leaving Tez in the dust. I can't believe this guy! This is definitely a hauling-butt kind of moment! How can he just *walk*?!

It's a foggy night, the gray haze making everything look blurry and unreal. It's still the witching hour too, so who knows what sort of otherworldly phantoms are swirling around this place, their spectral forms intermingling with the haze of night.

I run straight to the camp director's cabin. It's bigger than the other cabins and marked with the name GLADYS WINCHELHAUSER in hand-lettered red on the dark wooden door. Tez stops sharply behind me, his sneakers squeaking on the damp concrete. I hesitate for a moment before knocking.

What am I going to say? What does Gladys Winchelhauser know? What doesn't she know? What doesn't she *want* to know? I haven't talked to her at all really. It's not like she personally chatted with me when she excused us from the Bug Hut. But she seemed friendly enough, a short middle-aged woman in a Camp Sweetwater T-shirt, with eyeglasses that cover most of her face.

"Should I knock?" I ask Tez in a whisper.

"Who dares disturb the man behind the curtain?" he says.

"Ohhhhh, *The Wizard of Oz*. I get it. I hope Mrs. Winchelhauser doesn't have flying monkeys in there. Those monkeys skeeve the cheese out of me."

"Me too! I knew we were soul mates. I mean friends. I mean shut up Corryn whatever, *you're* a flying monkey."

Probably more to change the subject than anything else, Tez starts banging on the door. His fist echoes on the wood like a cannon blast booming in the night. "Attention, Mrs. Winchelhauser, the great and powerful!" he bellows. "Something is rotten in the state of Ohio!"

"You're really mixing your references, Tez."

"Forget it, Corryn. It's Chinatown!"

"What?"

"I don't know, just go with it." He bangs on the door again, even louder this time. Four rapid blasts like drums at the beginning of a punk song. 1-2-3-4!

Gladys Winchelhauser opens the door. At least I think it's her—the lighting is not good and she's lacking her signature glasses.

"What is the meaning of this?" she says. "Jones, Quinn—what are the two of you doing darkening my door at this most ungodly hour?"

I'm kind of surprised that she knows my name. Also, I had forgotten that Tez's last name is Jones.

"Um, yeah, well, here's the thing—" he says.

She cuts him off. She snaps on her eyeglasses and is now all business. "Do your counselors know where you are?"

"I mean, well, probably not," Tez says. "But listen! We—"

Gladys Winchelhauser cuts him off again. Tez's deafening door-poundage has roused the other camp staff in the adjacent cabins. Soon lights are popping on, one by one. More and more disheveled heads are sticking out of doors and windows.

"Jenny, be a dear," she says to one of them. "Go up to Oak and bring Gavin and Mary down to me. I would like to have a word with them."

I hear Tez audibly gulp.

"I don't think we need to get Gavin and Mary down here," I say. "Please hear us out. We really have some important . . . Tez, show her the locket."

Tez hands over the antique locket he took from the cellar. Well, he tries to hand it to her. She does not take it. She looks down her nose at it and says dryly, "You've come to give me costume jewelry. Just what I needed. How *ever* did you know?"

"It's Virginia Finch's," Tez says flatly.

"One of the missing campers! From 1883! There are beads, and their clothes, and, Mrs. Winchelhauser, there are *bones* down there," I add. "Other bodies!"

Winchelhauser's hue quickly turns a few notches toward chalk. Her face is positively bloodless.

"This is a very serious thing you're saying," she says.

"We know!" Tez and I yell in unison.

"Well, if this is true, I would have to call the police and . . ."

Just then, Mary and Gavin arrive on the path leading up to Winchelhauser's cabin. They're with Jenny, whoever that is, and they do not look happy.

"Oh, this git," Gavin mutters toward Tez.

"You're a git," Tez mutters back.

Mary says nothing, which is rare for her. She looks a little scared. I guess Gladys Winchelhauser is Scary Mary's kryptonite. Maybe she's afraid of being sent back to England. Ew, weird, am I having a moment of sympathy for Scary Mary?

"Enough," Winchelhauser says. "Gavin, were you aware that one of your charges has been out of his bunk?"

"No," Gavin says. "I had no idea. This chav basket is a right sneaky one, he is."

Winchelhauser raises a hand to shush him.

"And Miss Mary, were you aware that Quinn here has been galivanting about in the moonlight?"

"No ma'am," Mary says.

"We will address this lapse in the morning. Take them back with you now."

Tez and I look at each other incredulously. Is that it? She's going to sweep this under the rug? Go back to bed and deal with it in the morning?

"We're not going anywhere," Tez says.

"Yeah," I say. I take a step closer to Winchelhauser and push out my chest. "You said you were going to call the police. Well, good, call the police! I have a feeling Chief Wolpaw might like to see this." I pull the bone I took out of my sleeve and wave it about like a magic wand. I resist the urge to say *ta-da.*

"And what, pray tell, is that?" Winchelhauser says.

"It's a bone!" I say. "A human's bone!"

"A humerus, to be specific," Tez says.

"There is nothing funny about this, you git," Gavin says.

"Exactly," I say. "Nothing funny at all. Now about that call to the police . . ."

26

Wa-Pow!

Tez

Every inch of Camp Sweetwater flashes blue and red.

And it seems like every single camper is out of bed with their counselors. They crowd the paths that lead down from junior and senior camp. Corryn and I couldn't walk back to our cabins if we wanted to. Or if we were allowed.

"All right, I'm going to need you to go through this for me one more time," the detective says. She flips a page in her notebook, but backward instead of forward. A *detective.*

I sit on the bumper of a state highway patrol car.

Across the staff parking lot, Corryn sits on another. She has her own detective, a man in a boxy suit.

Tipping my head back, I look at my detective earnestly. "I know you're checking to make sure I got my story straight. And I swear to you, it's not going to change. We can show you where the pit is. The yearbooks are in the camp office. Mr. Ferdle at the public library in town can help you look at the old newspapers."

The detective arches her ginger brow. I think she probably doesn't appreciate smart alecks. This is like being back in school; I feel like I forgot everything I already learned about being cool from Corryn. I can't help it, though. This has all been so strange.

Because the first person to show up wasn't a police officer at all. Mrs. Winchelhauser didn't even call the police! Instead, this guy was a park ranger. He had a brown suit and a patch on his shoulder with a scenic view. And a ranger hat, which Corryn promised she would steal as soon as he was out of earshot.

As Corryn and I stood there, the ranger rolled the bone over and over in his hands. Mrs. Winchelhauser swore it had to belong to a deer. That this was just camp hijinks, and she'd only called because he could set us straight. These things, she told him, have a way of turning into ugly rumors if they're not addressed.

Everything was strange and creaky-quiet as the ranger rasped his hands on the bone. Corryn and I weren't allowed to talk. Scary Mary and Gavin stood behind us, their hands digging into our shoulders. It felt like a threat.

Watching Mrs. Winchelhauser's face, listening to her insist that this had to be nothing—it reminded me a lot of the day I asked her why they closed the camp so much. Her eyes didn't turn black. She wasn't possessed or anything. But she was sure—dead sure—that she didn't want me asking questions like that. That's exactly what she looked like as the ranger spoke to her.

"I'm sorry, ma'am," the park ranger finally said. His posture changed. He let the bone rest in both of his hands. Gently. "But I'm afraid these *are* human remains. We're going to need to call in the police."

Corryn lifted her chin and shouted, "That's what *we* told her!"

Then she made a little whimpering noise. Scary Mary's knuckles were almost white. She must have dug her fingers into Corryn's flesh hard. I didn't say anything, but I shifted my arm and rubbed my elbow against hers. I caught her gaze. Since ghosts and vampire devils and everything else seemed real, I tried telepathy. *It's going to be okay.*

Even though Mrs. Winchelhauser offered the phone in her office, the park ranger called the police on his radio. And I don't know the range on his radio, but he didn't just summon the police from Fan du Lac, although they showed up first: all four of them, including Chief Wolpaw.

Police cars with other town names painted on the side poured in, and after that, the state highway patrol, and then blue sedans with no markings at all. They all had their lights flashing, and some came with sirens. They silenced them once they realized that the remains weren't some brand-new camper still in his Keds.

They woke the whole camp, even the little kids in Bantam Camp. Curious kids peered toward us from the parking lot and the walking paths. They watched the police question me and Corryn, then mill around while the detectives questioned us separately.

And the thing is, we didn't tell the police about the faces in the fire, or about the lake trying to kill Corryn, or the way the devilwood froze time and forced us to watch the past.

Corryn and I looked at each other and agreed silently when Chief Wolpaw started asking questions. Telepathy must be a little bit real, because we told the same lie: we'd heard about the missing campers and decided to play detective.

That's all. We kept everything else to ourselves, because the rest didn't matter. The facts were the facts: we found the remains of Dorothy Duane, Virginia Finch, and Leigh Wade, and we brought back proof.

Chief Wolpaw said we couldn't be sure who we found, but that he would be glad to reopen that investigation. (He also told Mrs. Winchelhauser he met us for the first time at the library in town, where our junior camper selves were definitely not supposed to be, so I'm pretty sure that both our cabins have negative beads at this point.)

After that, they handed us over to a pair of detectives. One was a man with short brown hair and a crooked nose, like it had been broken once. The other was a woman with red hair and a perfect poker face. I thought for sure that she would talk to Corryn, but when they separated us, the female detective put a hand on my shoulder and led me away.

The whole time she questioned me, her face was

smooth. Not a hint of emotion, not even a clue whether she believed me or not. But she had to!

It's not like we could have *made up* a human bone. It's not like we came to camp with old-fashioned glasses, just waiting for a chance to find missing campers we didn't even know about until we got here. We didn't even know each other. We would have to be super geniuses to plot something like this with a stranger we hadn't even met.

My detective clicks and unclicks her pen. Somehow, even with all the whispering and rumbling and paper-cup crushing going on around us, that's the sound I hear. *Tick-tick-tick.* It reminds me of the dripping in the infirmary. My stomach rolls over, sick.

The camp obviously got to Mrs. Winchelhauser. It took control of Örn and the nurse, Miss Kortepeter. It possessed Bowl Cut and Ew and every bug in Ohio.

Tick. Tick. Tick.

I wonder, how fast does it work?

Who does it work on? And who—

"You can show us this cellar?" My detective sounds intrigued.

A tiny bubble of hope rises in my chest. I look up at her. "Yes. We can take you there right now. We don't even need flashlights! Although, flashlights would help! Also, canoes."

With one more click, my detective cracks the tiniest smile. It's the first expression she's made in half an hour. "I think Ranger Wescott can handle that. But thank you."

She closes her notepad and tells me to stay put. Then she walks across the staff parking lot, meeting her partner halfway in the middle. Standing close, they keep their voices low. I can't hear them.

But I see Corryn across the way. She nods at me and throws a thumbs-up. All of a sudden, all the camp employees start to move. They raise their voices. It almost sounds like the first day again, everybody being assigned to their camps with their counselors.

A couple of uniformed police collect me and Corryn, though. They round us up and stop to talk to Mrs. Winchelhauser. To make sure that we're not going anywhere, in case the detectives have more questions.

"Oh no," Mrs. Winchelhauser promises with a grim smile. "We'll be keeping quite a close eye on these two."

This pleases the cops, and they let us go. Mrs. Winchelhauser turns that smile on us and I shudder.

"Go on, children," she trills, "straight back to your cabins."

Somehow, she manages to make that sound like a threat. Corryn and I move, pressed shoulder to shoulder with each other. We have a lot to talk about—what her detective said, what mine said. Mostly, though, I'm relieved, and Corryn's drooping shoulders indicate that she feels the same way. As we start up the long path to Oak Camp, I whisper to her.

"I think they believed us," I say.

"Uh, duh. They kind of had to," she replies. Her brashness is back; it lights her up from the inside. "Did you see me whip out that bone? Wa-pow!"

And like my detective, I finally crack my first smile of the night.

Corryn

The campers and the counselors march back to their cabins, a sleepy, somber middle-of-the-night processional no one expected.

Is it even the middle of the night anymore? With all the excitement I've lost track of time. It has a way of slowing down and speeding up on nights like this.

Who am I kidding? There has *never* been a night like this. It might be almost morning for all I can tell.

I ask Tez what time it is as we walk up the path toward our cabins. He checks his watch by the scant moonlight.

"It's almost dawn," he says. "Sun will be up in a few minutes. No one is going back to bed."

"As if anyone could possibly sleep." I elbow Tez in the ribs.

"Stop," he says, but he giggles a little.

"Oh, does ickle Tez have a wee little tickle spot for the tickle bug there?" I say, busting out my British accent. I reach over to get him right in the tickle zone.

"Stop," he says again. He catches my hand and squashes the tickle bug brutally.

I stare at him. "What the heck, Tez?"

"Stop and look, Corryn! Over there! The Old Lifeguard is doing something weird, even for him."

Indeed, the Old Lifeguard is standing off the side of the path, staring up at the moon with his arms outstretched. Tez is watching, scratching his head. I want to get a closer look. I try to walk quietly, tiptoeing across the grass. But Tez clods along behind me and tramples a bunch of sticks. Our cover is blown.

"Oh, hey, Old Lifeguard," I say. "What are you doing?"

He answers me but doesn't take his eyes off the sky. His head is leaned back; he looks like a human scarecrow pointed at the stars. "I'm doing something I have wanted to do for a long time but couldn't until tonight. Thank you for this, by the way." He turns toward us, and I see gold hanging from his hand. The locket. We gave it to Mrs. Winchelhauser, but now the Old Lifeguard has it swinging from his fingers.

Tez asks, "Is that . . . ?"

"I haven't felt this close to Ginny in a long, long while," the Old Lifeguard says, cutting him off.

"Wait, Ginny?" Tez says.

"Virginia Finch, duh," I whisper. That's how you know it's really late. I'm quicker on the uptake than Encyclopedia Jones over there.

"How did you get that?" Tez asks. "That's evidence now and it has to be handled properly in order to ensure—"

"I took it off Gladys' desk. It was easy. Walked right in there. No one saw me. People see what they want to see and flat-out ignore what doesn't suit their eyes."

"We never did catch your name," I say.

The Old Lifeguard sighs. "They used to call me

Finchy. I came here to work the year Ginny enrolled; our mother was overprotective. She wanted me to watch over her."

"Virginia Finch is your brother?" I ask. "I mean, you're her sister? Sheesh, I'm tired. You know what I mean! It's been a long night."

"It's been a long night for a long time now. I've been away for too long. Away from Ginny, away from everything. I could never get her out, but you did. And now it's time to go home. I failed a hundred years ago, but I hope I made up for that tonight."

Stunned, Tez and I share a look.

"It's not over, you know," Finchy says suddenly. His voice is thinner, almost a whisper. "They're not happy. You took something that belonged to them. Whatever you do, stay out of the deep."

"What do you mean?" Tez asks.

Instead of answering, Finchy looks up to the sky and closes his eyes. The first light of day breaks through the canopy of trees. As the sunlight strikes him, he starts to change. His gray hair regains its youthful color, and his shaggy-old-man cut reshapes into carefully combed waves.

His mustache dissolves, retreating into his upper

lip like spaghetti being slurped off a fork. His clothes change too, his red lifeguard's jacket becoming a collarless shirt, crisscrossed with thin leather suspenders that hold up slim trousers. The age slips from his face, until he looks just like he did in the yearbook.

And then the breeze carries a girl's voice on it. It's so full of joy, I feel it in my bones. She cries out, "Charles!"

The Old Lifeguard—Finchy—turns and melts into a smile. I grab Tez's arm and dig my fingers in hard. There, at the edge of the tree line, stands a girl in a high-necked dress. No. Three girls. The other two are laughing behind their hands, whispering impossible secrets to each other. I'd say I can't believe my eyes, but it would be a lie. I've seen too much in the last week.

"Do you . . . ," I whisper.

Tez nods, whispering back, "Yeah."

Neither of us moves. We just watch. Watch as an impossibly young, impossibly happy Charles Finch taunts his sister. Some things between siblings never change.

"You forgot this," Finchy says, holding the locket out for her to see.

The girl . . . Virginia . . . dashes forward to claim it. Twice, he pulls it out of her reach, then finally hands it over. She loops it around her neck quickly, then beams up at Finchy. "Wherever did you find it? I looked everywhere!"

"You'll never guess," he says. And then he takes her under his arm and pulls her in close. They don't spare a glance for us. It's like we're not there anymore; like *we're* the ghosts. Together, they walk toward the other girls. The girls loop their arms, falling into step with Finchy and Virginia. The four of them walk off the path, into the tree line, and disappear into the mist.

As soon as they're gone, we come back to our senses.

"Don't go," Tez shouts. "You have to explain!"

The wind is cool off the lake. It washes over us, and I put a hand on Tez's shoulder. With a squeeze, I say, "Buddy, I think we know. They finally get to go home. And the vampire devils? Not happy about it."

As if to confirm it, a low roll of thunder spills through the sky. And the waves on Camp Sweetwater, just for a moment, churn and glow green. Mist rises up, creeping like long, skeletal fingers, toward the shore. The color fades; the thunder silences.

Oh yeah. We know.

27
Super Smoky Camp Baloney

June 17, 1983

Corryn

It's been three days, and no one is telling us anything.

It's driving Tez crazy. (I'm not super happy about it either, but man, is he cranky!)

Across the lake, yellow crime scene tape flickers between the trees. We see it when we go to outdoor activities. It taunts us during swimming. It sneers all through nature encounter, nature hike, and nature appreciation.

One of the senior campers fished enough of the tape from the lake to wear as a headband. He jogged up and down the shore with it until he got sent to Winchelhauser's office. Of course, the crime scene itself is completely off-limits. We're not even allowed to take out the canoes because we might get close to it!

For her part, Winchelhauser insists that we "carry on with vigor and good cheer." We meet this with universal eye rolls. She has all of our counselors remind us about a hundred times a day that we must let the police do their job and not panic about an ancient accident.

Puh-leeze.

She actually gives a speech at the flagpole, insisting that we continue to behave in a manner consistent with the "spirit of Sweetwater." I want to ask which spirit she means, exactly. The evil ones that live in the lake? The ones Tez and I set free, when nobody else could?

I don't, and Winchelhauser carries on. Some of the campers are even buying her super smoky summer camp baloney. They're back to worrying about earning beads for color war. That's weeks away, and there's a crime scene in rowing distance!

Tez won't give up on it, of course. When he wants to know something, he can't be distracted. Plus, I'm pretty sure he never cared about beads to begin with. Which is good, because both of our cabins are sitting at about negative twenty-five.

Braids and Hairspray are really ticked at me about that, and I'm sure Tez is taking some grief from Nostrils and Knees. Hopefully no one kicks him in the face again. I'm feeling kind of protective of the little dude. If they start something? Wa-pow!

Now that we're done with breakfast this morning, Tez and I are on a mission to find a newspaper. We want to see how this thing is being reported. We want to see what Winchelhauser isn't telling us, which I'm sure is a lot!

I remember seeing Örn with a paper a few times, presumably just for the sports pages. That's why we pick him as our prime target. We make our way to the tennis courts and find them strangely empty. I guess Örn ran out of balls.

His duffel bag is sitting there though, labeled PROPERTY OF ÖRN ODINSON. It's just hanging out on a bench like, *Hey, check me out. Maybe there is a newspaper in me. Maybe I smell like Absorbine Jr. Maybe both! Come find out!*

"I am Örn Odinson, son of Odin, ruler of worlds,"

Tez says to me in a weird voice. Before I can ask him what he means, he goes back to his normal voice and says, "You be lookout."

"*You* be lookout," I say.

"Fine, we'll both be lookout."

"That's not how lookouts work; one of us has to get the paper!" I say. "I don't think we really need a lookout anyway. It's not grand larceny to steal the news. Information wants to be free! Besides, we're just borrowing it."

"Oh yeah, we'll totally return it, just like we did that bike," he says, a brow arched.

I give Tez a look. We're still totally going to return that bike. I haven't forgotten. Since he's being a weenie, I run up to the duffel bag and whip it open. It *does* smell like Absorbine Jr. Gross.

"Check it out!" Tez says from right beside me. There, sitting on top of a moist towel, is a copy of the *Fan du Lac Spectre*. It's folded so we don't see the headline, only some minor stories about college sports teams and something about a local guy who has seen *Star Wars* four hundred times. I grab the paper.

"What does it say?" Tez asks.

But before I can answer, I hear a voice shouting

from across the courts. "Hey!" Örn says. "What are you doing in my bag?"

"See," Tez says. "Someone should have been lookout."

"Shut up and run!" I say. I tuck the paper under my shirt and book it back to camp.

"I thought your ankle was sprained!" I hear Örn yell.

"All better, thanks!" I shout back, not breaking my stride.

I sprint back to Oak Camp.

Tez toddles after me, still doing his monkey walk. Turning to jog backward in front of him, I say, "Seriously, how slow are you?"

"I have to be," Tez says, like he's admitting something. Something in his expression changes. It's thoughtful and scared and just muddled up with a lot of feelings. He takes a deep breath. Then he totally admits something.

"I have this heart thing. I could have a heart attack if I'm not careful. I have to be really careful."

"What? No way!" I start to shove him. Then I stop, because he doesn't look like he's joking. Jeez, what if I hit him and set it off? I put my hands on my hips and walk up to him, almost nose to nose. "What kind of thing?"

He rolls his shoulders. "I just can't get super excited."

"Like investigating ghosts and vampire devils and falling in cellars and . . . Tez! What the hecky darn, man?! You could have died! But like, different died!"

There's quiet a moment. Then Tez plasters his sweaty, stinky hand over my face. It's totally a me move. I'm both proud and grossed out. "That's why I don't do sports when everybody else does. But I can manage it. I know what I'm doing. It's just, no one believes I know what I'm doing."

Skeptically, I raise an eyebrow. Usually when somebody insists they know what they're doing, it's because they don't know diddley. But Tez is a walking set of Funk and Wagnalls . . . and he's my friend. I say, "You better."

"Don't tell anybody, okay?"

He looks seriously desperate. This means something to him, and, well, it's not hard to keep my mouth shut. We didn't tell the park ranger, Winchelhauser, the town police, or the detectives about half the stuff that really happened. I can keep this secret too—while I keep an eye on him, just in case.

"Who would I tell?" I ask carelessly, to make him feel like it's no big deal. "The only thing Hairspray cares about is getting her bangs closer to God."

"Okay, good." He opens my cabin door and waits for me to walk in first, like a big, dumb gentleman. If he thinks I'm not going to grill him about this, he's crazy. Except, when I get inside, Braids, Ew, and Hairspray are there. I just promised not to say anything, and I'm not happy about it.

"Oh, hey, what's up?" I say. "Cool, cool, yeah, nothing."

"Boys aren't supposed to be in the girls' cabins," Hairspray says, looking past me, at Tez.

"Oh well! There he is! Nobody's on fire!" Waving my hands, I try to distract her from this bead-losing infraction of epic proportions. The paper under my shirt crinkles suspiciously. I mean, not to me. I know it's a newspaper. But Braids gets super interested.

"What have you got under your shirt there, killer?" she asks.

"Nothing!" I say. "Just like, normal under-shirt stuff that people have under their shirts all of the time."

"Oh, quit it," Tez says. "Just let me see the paper already."

I retrieve the slightly sweaty newspaper from under my shirt and hand it to Tez.

"Ew," Ew says. "All that drama for a newspaper. Who even reads newspapers?"

Tez ignores her and spreads the paper across my bed. We don't have to look far to find an article about our crime scene. It's big-headline, page-one stuff. "Bodies Found at Camp Sweetwater May Be Linked to Century-Old Mystery."

"Now we're talking," Tez says. He rubs his hands together.

"Ew," says Ew.

Tez starts to read aloud, which is weird. But it's even weirder because his face twists up into an uncomfortable grimace, as if the words are causing him severe physical discomfort. Tez is capital-*F* furious. F-U-R-I-O-U-S. He gives running commentary on the article too.

"What? No. Come on!" He goes on, "I'm going to have to write a strongly worded letter to the editor about this. *Strongly worded.* It says that the girls' bones were found in a 'previously unknown stockyard.' A stockyard?! How could a mysterious stockyard show up out of nowhere? That's crazy! Those were not animal bones. We're talking about a charnel pit, people."

"What's a charnel pit?" Braids asks.

"A furtive storage pit for human bones," Tez says.

"Ew," says everyone.

Tez scowls. "A *very* strongly worded letter."

"Are you, like . . . sure those were human bones?" Ew asks. Her voice is quieter than usual, and she nibbles on one of her fingernails. "Like, really sure?"

"Cross my heart," I say.

Tez adds, "We almost died."

Tez

"Hey," Bowl Cut says, sticking his gleaming pate into the girls' cabin.

Pate means scalp, and I've never had a reason to use it until now. Trust me, there has never been a pate-ier pate than the round, incandescent bulb of Bowl Cut's shaved head. I bet we could use it to redirect sunlight to create an intense beam capable of setting things on fire. Not that Corryn and I know *anything* about that.

Braids stands up and yelps, "We already have one boy in here!"

In response, Bowl Cut staggers in, shoved along by Knees and Nostrils. "Now you have four!"

The cabins aren't that big when there are four people crammed into them. Stuff in four more, and it's what my mom would call *cozy*.

To be fair though, Braids, Hairspray, and Ew do their best to smoosh into a single bunk, leaning away from us like we have leprosy. Which would be pointless anyway, because leprosy isn't actually that contagious. It just has a bad reputation.

Nostrils leans against the empty bunk. I'm pretty sure he's been practicing this lean. It's a lot smoother than it was on day one, when he slid off the wall and landed on his derriere. "Soooo, what's going on, ladies?"

With a quick look at each other, Braids and Hairspray giggle at the same time. Then Hairspray says, "Tez was reading us the newspaper."

"No, for real," says Knees in disbelief.

With that, Corryn officially loses her Cheez Whiz. Hands on hips, she glowers at my cabinmates. "That's really what we were doing! That trashy town paper says that we found a bunch of *animal bones*. They're trying to pretend like those three missing girls were the only people down there!"

Bowl Cut gets even paler, if possible, and sits down on a bunk. "Wait. There were *more*?"

With her nose in the air, Braids says, "I'm still not even convinced there were *any*."

Shaking a fist at her, Corryn asks, "Do you wanna have a chat with my convincer?"

"Stop!" I shout. Yikes, that was loud. And we really aren't supposed to be in the girls' cabin, not that it matters. We have no beads left to lose. I guess it might be hypothetically interesting to see how low the negative balance can go, but . . .

"I can prove there were people," I say. "And when I do, then . . . maybe we have something else to tell you."

Everybody murmurs curiously, even Corryn. I duck across the path and into my cabin. There, hanging on the end of my bunk, is my canteen. Snatching it by the strap, I run back across.

Scary Mary and Gavin are nowhere to be seen. That might be a good thing (maybe they quit and we'll get new, better counselors?) or a bad thing (they might be stealthily hiding, waiting to cut us all down at once).

The police took the arm bone Corryn found. And Finchy disappeared with the locket. But we still have one piece of proof. Uncapping my canteen, I tip it out over my outstretched palm. Water spills on the floor, and in seconds, it's already seeping between the boards.

"Hey!" Braids and Hairspray scream at the same time, and then Knees imitates them, echoing it back. I'm not entirely sure a fight isn't going to break out, so I hurry.

"It's just water," I tell them as two cool, stony bones fall into my hand. "But this is an opposable thumb. Only humans have them. And we found them down there. In the *charnel* pit."

Swaying forward to look, Ew looks green as she murmurs, "Ew."

Our cabinmates press close to get a better look. They kind of have to take my word for it that it's a thumb. But it's bones; even they can't deny that. Bowl Cut knits his brows, rubbing his hands against his dirty knees.

"What's the other thing you have to tell us?" he asks slowly.

I was about to go back to the very first day, but Corryn jumps in. "The camp is cursed. That story you told about the vampire devils, Nostrils? The ones who want to devour us? Yeah. It's true."

"Oh, please," Braids scoffs.

Hairspray shakes her head. "Nuh-uh, not even."

With a huge snort, Nostrils almost slides off the bunk, forgetting all his cool. "Dude, that's a campfire story! My brother told me it! They told it when *he* went to camp in *Indiana*. It didn't even happen here!"

Ew doesn't leap in with a protest. Instead, she clears her throat and points at the floor. "Um."

We all look down. We look down just in time to see the water beading into shimmery threads. It forms itself together, rolling like mercury on the wood. It's not normal; it looks alive. The rest of it just soaked in, but this swirls. Then slowly, it spreads out, taking shape.

My stomach gurgles in terrible anticipation. Out of reflex, I reach out and catch hold of Corryn's arm. Her skin is warm, and I'm glad, because a chill runs through me again. But my stomach settles when we step closer together.

Whatever this is, we'll handle it. Just like we did the faces in the fire.

Then the message appears. The water glimmers and sparkles and spells out

THANK YOU

before it drains away into the wood. It leaves nothing behind but a splash pattern.

The cabin suddenly feels too full and too quiet, all at the same time. It's all out there now. Corryn and I aren't the only ones who know what's happening at Camp Sweetwater. What's *really* happening, that is.

I look to Corryn, giving her arm a squeeze. She nods back in reply. It's not just us now, not alone, not anymore.

"How do you like them apples?" she asks our cabin-mates. Her expression dares them to argue.

But instead, Ew raises her hand. Her voice is soft, and her big green eyes seem to fill up half her face. She looks like one of those weird paintings, little bodies, big heads, of kids crying over teddy bears and stuff. I feel a little pang for her. I don't know what I expect her to say, but it's definitely not this:

"What if," she starts, then looks to Bowl Cut. "What if some of us have also seen stuff?"

"Yeah, what if haunted things have happened to us too?" Bowl Cut asks.

I feel a spark pass through us. It's like little strikes of lightning; it zings between Bowl Cut and Ew, and right through me and Corryn. There's *more*? There's stuff we don't even know yet?

"Maybe we should all sit down," I say.

Then Corryn says as she drops down next to me, "And you guys should start at the beginning."

Because for the rest of camp, we're in this together.

THE END

(For now!)